KINGPIN WIFEYS

SEASON 3, VOLUME 9

BY K. ELLIOTT

Contents

KINGPIN WIFEYS III,

PART 3: HAPPY BIRTHDAY

Agent Daniels took a step back after realizing that it was Jada behind the wheel of the car. He banged on the window as agents approached the passenger side of the car. One agent stood near the front passenger side and the other stood at the rear near the trunk.

Daniels tapped on the window with a flashlight and said, "Turn off the car."

Jada turned off the ignition and Daniels said, "What the hell is going on?"

Jada lowered the window. The wipers sloshing as buckets of rain fell from the sky. The wipers were freaking her out as her mind drifted back to the day Lani was murdered. She hated those damn wipers. She hated that it was raining. Then there were sirens. A chopper overhead sounded like an eggbeater.

Daniels ordered Dumas and Mackins to retreat. Something wasn't adding up. Why was Jada here? Had Jada set him up? The agents walked swiftly back to their automobiles. Daniels climbed into a wintergreen Cherokee. Agent Dumas sat on the other side, biting his nails.

Dumas said, "What the fuck is going on, man?" He closed his eyes and took deep breaths trying to calm himself down.

"I don't know," Daniels said.

The shrilling sound of a siren drew near. Daniels was about to speed away when Agent Mackins, who was parked directly behind Daniels in a blue Chevy Impala, honked his horn.

Daniels lowered his window and said, "What the fuck is going on?"

"I'm stuck in the mud, bro."

Sure enough, the wheels were gaining traction. Daniels and Dumas vaulted from their vehicle to advance the Impala from the muddy ditch.

Jada glanced over her shoulders as she yapped on the cellphone. Daniels removed his nine millimeter, cocked the hammer, then aimed at Jada's car.

Dumas took hold of Daniels's hand, trying to seize the weapon. "What the fuck? Are you crazy?"

Daniels turned to him and frowned, "Don't you see? Don't you see that she gave us up?"

"If that's the case, you damn sure don't want to kill her if they're on the way."

He lowered his weapon.

Agent Mackins honked the horn inside the Impala again and said, "Hey, you need to help me. We need to get the hell out of here."

Daniels and Dumas rocked the car until it gained traction.

When Daniels hopped back into the car, they were barricaded by two huge black SUVs. Eight FBI and DEA agents jumped out of the car with their weapons drawn.

"Drop your weapons and put your hands up where I can see them!" Daniels put his hands on his head and said to Jason Levy, one of the agents that he'd had a relationship with, "Hey, what's going on? I don't understand."

"Barry, just do what we tell you to do."

Inside the FBI office, Jada sat in a chair surrounded by four FBI agents: a Hispanic woman, two white men, and a black man. The Hispanic woman, Elaine Garcia, was a doll-faced woman with flawless skin. Elaine wore a tight blue pinstriped pantsuit that revealed her Dominican curves. Jada would absolutely fuck her under the right circumstances. The men looked hideous. And the black guy was the worst of the three. His name was Jacob Levy. He was a thirty-five-year-old man with leathery skin and keloids sprinkled on the back of his neck. Levy wore a cheap gray suit and ugly brown shoes.

He eyed Jada. "It's Ms. Simone? Is that your last name?"

"Yes."

He grabbed a chair and sat down right beside her. Garlic oozed from his skin.

"Ms. Simone?"

She scanned the room. Interrogation rooms always seemed to be cold, and Jada wondered if it was a tactic to make the room as uncomfortable as possible. Jacob Levy was staring her right in the face. The garlic smell was becoming unbearable.

"Yes, Mr. Levy?"

"So your attorney set you up with a deal where you would give up Barry Daniels. We certainly do appreciate that. We want to get rid of all the corruption in the Atlanta division of the F.B. I. It makes us all look bad; you know what I mean? But you didn't get him to talk. Why didn't he talk?"

Jada had met with the FBI in Birmingham right after she'd switched cars with Shantelle and they'd wired her. She was supposed to get Barry Daniels to talk, but she knew that he would be alarmed when he saw her. She didn't really think she could get him in trouble, but she wanted to scare him. The goal was to get him to leave her the fuck alone.

"But it's like he knew something wasn't right. Like he wasn't expecting you to be in that car. And why didn't he call you one time on your cell phone. I'm curious. As soon as he saw you, he tried to flee."

"How am I supposed to know that?"

"I find it odd that you told him that you were going to be a courier and he didn't call you one time. I want to know why he blackmailed you and how he was able to get you to go along with his plans. Must've had some really serious shit to hold over your head."

Jada wondered if this motherfucker was serious. Was he trying to get her locked up or was he just simply trying to show off in front of these white folks? There was always that one nigga that was trying to do his job far beyond expectations. A super employee is what she liked to call those types.

Elaine Garcia interrupted and said, "Ms. Simone has been through a lot."

Jacob Levy crossed his arms then rubbed the back of his head, bringing attention to those ugly-ass keloids. Jada wanted to throw up.

"I know she has, but one has to wonder why did he pick her. Does Ms. Simone have a supplier in Texas herself? Is she involved with this network? Why did he come to her and ask *her* to make a trip down to Houston to bring back the coke? We need to find out who she knows. How did he know that she had a supplier, a connect?"

Peter Sandford, a tall, white agent with curly brown hair, said, "I'm with Jacob on this one. Since we got her here, we need to find out what she knows."

"Can I call my attorney?"

"You can, but you're not going to get the opportunity to clear yourself of any wrong doing. Today is the day for the interview. Today is the only chance that you will have to come clean."

"Meaning?"

"We tried to reach your attorney and he's in court today."

"So we can't have this interview tomorrow?"

"Absolutely not," Levy said.

Jada huffed and then said, "I've already told you that my ex-boyfriend was a D-Boy. His friend Black worked with Barry Daniels and Daniels was certain that I knew Black's connect, but I didn't. He threatened to expose me and Black's relationship to my ex." Jada started to cry.

"So you agreed to go along with Daniels because he knew that you had slept with Black? You really want us to believe that?"

"I don't care if you believe it or not. It's the truth."

"Okay," Levy coughed, "why didn't you want him to find out?"

"Because they were friends and I knew this would have hurt Shamari."

"Were they best friends?"

"No, but they were good friends. Very close."

"And Daniels told you the only way that he would not tell this story to your ex was for you to let him know when you were bringing drugs back so he could take them?"

"Yes. Barry Daniels had made up his mind that I was a courier and so I had to go along with it. Though I know nothing about drug dealing."

"Where were you going to ge t the drugs from if you didn't know the connect?"

Jada was sweating and thinking to herself, this house nigga motherfucker had tripped her up. He'd just backed her into a corner with a question that she didn't have the answer for.

A long silence.

House-nigga Levy asked again. "So, where were you going to get the drugs from?"

"I don't know. I made it up. I told them that I would get them so he would get off my back. I contacted my attorney and he contacted you to get me a deal to give up Daniels."

"What about Fresh's plug?"

"What plug?" Jada bite her lip.

"You didn't think we knew about Fresh and the fact that he's wanted down in Houston?"."

"Okay."

Sandford said, "Jada, why don't you tell us about Fresh because if Barry Daniels decides to tell us anything about you, we're going to pick you up. Do you really think an FBI agent is going to keep his mouth shut?"

"I don't know shit."

Garcia interrupted and said, "Look, Jada, you're free to go. Let's just hopes this doesn't come back on you."

"Look, I gave you Daniels. Doesn't that count for anything?"

"Let's just hope you're not involved," Levy said, then rubbed those nasty-ass bumps again.

* * * * *

Fresh's doorbell rang. He dashed into the guest bedroom to view the security monitor. Two black women stood in front of his home. He tiptoed to the door and then asked, "Who is it?"

"Starr."

He opened the door and found that Starr was standing there with a gorgeous, brown-skinned, young woman wearing fitted white jeans and heels with a T-shirt. Fresh would definitely fuck the young bitch. He invited them in.

"This is my assistant, Brooke," Starr said. Fresh nodded and wondered what in the hell were they here for. Starr knew he was on the lam. Did something happen to Jada? He was still confused about why Shantelle had brought back the work in Jada's car instead of the car he had assigned her. She had simply said that Jada told her to drive the car and she would explain later.

Fresh offered them a seat.

"We won't be here long."

"What brings you here?" Then he cut his eye at Brooke and decided she was probably silly as hell at that age. "Where is Jada?"

"She's home. She told us to come here to meet you."

"She told you to come over here?"

Starr nodded, "She did."

Fresh rubbed his chin. "I don't understand."

"She doesn't want to talk to you over the phone." Starr dug into her purse and handed him a piece of loose-leaf notebook paper with an address and a phone number scribbled in marker ink. "Meet her at the address on the paper."

Fresh trembled as he held onto the loose-leaf notebook paper. He stood and paced.

"What the fuck is going on, Starr?"

"I don't know, Fresh. I've told you everything that Jada has told me. She said that she was going to tell me later."

"Is this a setup? What the fuck? You know PoPo is looking for me, Starr."

"Not Jada's style."

Fresh thought about how hurt Jada had been when she had found out about his baby mother, but he still believed that Jada wouldn't hurt him.

Fresh smiled and said, "Thanks, Starr! Thank you so much for coming over and thanks for delivering the message." He looked at Brooke and said, "Nice to meet you." And stole a look at the young girl's ass.

"Likewise."

Such a proper little bitch he thought.

Fresh threw on a pair of Jordans, some jeans, and a T-shirt. Then he hopped into his car and drove to the address listed on the paper. A law building with a parking deck. He dialed the number of the phone on the paper just like Jada had asked.

"Where are you?" Jada asked.

"I'm at the address that was on the paper."

"Is there anyone following you?

He spotted a dark blue Honda Accord and a black Dodge Ram. Both the cars had tailed him from his house.

"Where do you want me to go?"

"Okay, you see a black man standing outside, wearing a dingy Young Jeezy shirt standing with a sign that reads overnight parking?"

"I see him."

"Give him five dollars to enter the parking garage then drive to the third level."

Fresh drove up to the man and the man said, "Twenty dollars for parking."

"I thought it was five."

"You just missed the five-dollar cutoff. There is going to be a concert tonight and you know how they do, my brother." The man smiled and then said, "You driving this nice-ass ride. I know you ain't tripping 'bout no petty-ass fifteen extra dollars."

Fresh was driving the BMW X6 that he'd offered to Jada; the one that she turned down.

Fresh peeled off a twenty-dollar bill and passed it to the man.

The man smiled then the parking lot arm raised and Fresh eased into the urine-soaked parking deck. behind a Kia Sport and circled around until he reached the third floor. He parked in a spot that was marked for compact cars.

Jada called and he answered, "Hello?"

"Where are you?" he asked.

I'm across from you, I'm in a white BMW."

"A what?"

"Starr's car."

"Okay, I see you."

He sprang from his car and walked over, climbing into the passenger side of the car.

Jada's weave was disheveled and she wasn't wearing any makeup. She appeared as she'd been crying all night. Fresh had never seen her look this bad.

He hugged and asked, "What the fuck is going on?"

"Too much shit. I don't know where to begin."

"Why'd you want me to come here?"

"Fresh, I don't know. I mean someone can be following you. I don't know who to trust. My life could be in danger. Your life could be in danger. I just thought this was the safest place for us to meet." Jada rambled for the next five minutes. She wasn't making a lot of sense to him. He needed her to calm down and talk slowly.

"What's going on, baby?" He held her hand and made eye contact with her. This was his way of letting her know that he was here with her and whatever they were going to face, they would face it together.

She took a deep breath. "Please don't repeat what I'm about to tell you."

 "I promise."

"Before Black was murdered, he was working with an FBI agent."

"What do you mean?"

"Not like that. The guy was taking shit from D-Boys and giving it to Black. Black was selling the shit."

"Why was he doing that?"

"I have no idea."

"Damn! Black was working with the police? Why in the fuck would he trust them? You think he told?"

"No," Jada said. She was furious. She was trying to tell him something and all he could do was worry about himself.

"What does this have to do with me?"

"The F.B.I. killed your connect and gave the drugs to Black."."

"What? This sounds like *The Wire* or *Power* or some shit."

"This is real life, baby! I couldn't make this up if I tried."

"I don't understand. So Black took the work and sold it and that's how he was able to leave that money for Shamari?"

"Yes."

"But what the fuck does this have to do with me?"

Jada looked away and although she knew that Fresh had cheated on her with his son's mother, there was no way that she was about to admit that she had slept with Black. She knew that he would not be as forgiving to her as she was to him. That was just the way the world worked. Women were always slut-shamed for being free with their bodies.

"What are you leaving out?" Fresh asked.

"Barry Daniels approached me a few weeks ago and he wanted to know when you were going to bring more coke back to Atlanta."

"Who the fuck is Barry Daniels?"

"The FBI dude."

"How the fuck does he know about me? Unless somebody told him!" Fresh yelled.

"Perhaps he'd seen you with Black. I believe he raided your house that time with the guns. You remember the case that you paid Joey Turch to make go away?"

A bum wearing a Peyton Manning jersey wandered up to the side of the window and tapped the glass. "Can you give me a dollar, my brother? I promise I'm going to get something to eat. I don't even drink if that's what you're thinking."

The stench of Old English exploded from his mouth. Fresh said, "Give me that Newport behind your ear and I'll give you this twenty."

The exchange was made and the happy bum said, "Thanks, my brother."

"Mind if I smoke?" Fresh asked Jada.

"You don't smoke cigarettes."

"I do now."

Fresh lit the Newport and blew out a smoke ring. "So this Barry, this Daniels guy, wanted to know when the work was coming back?"

"Yes, and he blackmailed me and said that he was going to charge me with conspiracy if I didn't tell him, but you know I would never let him know shit."

"So is that why you met up with Shantelle in Birmingham?"

"Yeah."

"She told me that you wanted to switch cars and that you would tell us all about it later, but that it was for the best."

"Yes, I did."

"And you did that because…"

"I'd gone to Joey Turch's office to make a payment for Shamari and Barry Daniels's name came up. Turch said he was bad news and I agreed. He wanted to know how I knew him and I'd told him what he was trying to do to me. He called the FBI and told the proper people and we set up a sting operation and I met with the FBI in Birmingham right after I exchanged cars with Shantelle."

"But you didn't have the product. Shantelle did."

"Yes, that was the point."

"So…"

"When Daniels pulled the car over, he thought it was Shantelle but it was me inside a wired up car. They wanted me to get Daniels to talk about drugs, but he became suspicious."

"Damn, that was cold."

"I was stupid."

"Why?"

"I did all of this for a man that doesn't love me."

"I love you, Jada."

"Cut the bullshit, Fresh."

He inhaled the cigarette. "So you didn't want to meet me because you thought that you might be being watched?"

"No, because the Feds questioned the shit out of me, and they asked me about you. They know that you are in Atlanta and are on the run for a double murder."

"How did they know that?"

"I don't know that, but Barry Daniels knew that too."

"He did?"

"And that lets me know it wasn't Black because Black had been murdered before you went on the run."

Fresh said, "Damn."

"What are you going to do?"

"I don't know. I was going to turn myself in after I got rid of my supply."

"You need to go pack your shit up and move."

"That's for sure."

He looked at her and he couldn't believe that she had put herself at risk. He leaned into her and tried to steal a kiss and she pushed him away.

He frowned and she said, "Go and do what you got to do so you can put this behind you. So you can get out to be with your family."

"No kiss for me?"

"No, Fresh."

He said, "Thanks for everything. You are a G."

She smiled and said, "You need to move right now, in the middle of the night if you have to."

"I will. Thanks, Jada."

"One cherry Danish," A tall, slender, redheaded cashier named Danny yelled. Then he said to Ava, "That will be two dollars and twelve cents. Would you like a latte to go with your Danish, ma'am?"

Ava stood in front of the counter of the Octaine coffeehouse and skimmed through her purse, searching _for twelve cents. She finally spotted a dime and two pennies. She handed the man the money and he handed her the Danish. Before she left, she decided that she needed a napkin.

She turned and gathered a few napkins and that's when she heard sixteen gunshots ring out. Everyone in the coffee shop hit the floor. After the shooting, Ava ran outside and she spotted the holes in her car. She cried before dropping the Danish and running back inside to call the police. It had to be them, she thought; t. The men that were looking for her in North Carolina were here and they knew where she was. She would have to get the fuck out of Atlanta.

Meeka inched toward Q and his eyes traveled her whole body. She had milky skin and her breasts were ample. Her kitty was neatly shaven. He hated to admit that he was aroused.. What the hell was he doing? Why was he looking at her like that? She was a very attractive woman, good-looking woman, but this was his ex's sister. He focused on her tiny feet with magenta nail polish. She walked toward him.

 "Fuck me, Q. I want to find out what the big deal about Q is. I know you have money, but can you fuck? Probably not. Rich dudes can't fuck, but a broke-ass thug will fuck the shit out of you. Real talk."

Seconds later, she was in his face, so close that he smelled Hennessy bursting from her mouth. He stepped back and she took hold of his hand and placed it on her ass.

"You want it," she said.

He held her soft ass for a moment. Meeka was not his type, but her body was alluring. She placed her hand on his manhood. Seconds later, she collapsed to her knees, nuzzling on his balls through his sweatpants. He pushed her head back.

She frowned, "What's wrong?"

"You know I'm in love with your sister."

"If you loved her, you would be with her right now. And where was she when you needed someone to get you out?" Meeka stood. "You're a weak motherfucka. You running around here chasing a bitch that don't even want yo' ass."

Q's eyes squished together. "You're talking about your sister."

"That bitch ain't my sister. Matter of fact, where the fuck is my money?"

Q pointed to the bag of money.

Meeka walked into the living room, picked up her clothes off the sofa, and was dressed in three minutes. Then she bolted.

* * * * *

Jada stared at the security app on her iPhone. Fresh stood outside, rocking from one foot to another. What the fuck was he doing at her door? Didn't she just tell him that they were onto his ass and that he should move? She'd lied for him and now this dumb motherfucker was standing outside like he wasn't wanted for a homicide. She opened the door and

22

invited him in, but didn't offer him a seat. She stood with her hands on her hip. She was wearing her gym clothes; her head was wrapped and she was prepared to get a good workout, but now he was here.

"What do you want?" she said.

"Damn, girl! That's how you go to the gym?"

"What are you talking about?"

"Tight clothes and shit."

"These are called leggings. This is what women wear to the gym."

"With hashtag that-ass-though on the back of your ass?"

Jada folded her arms across her chest and narrowed her eyes. "Look, Fresh, I picked them up on an Instagram boutique. I thought they were cute, so I bought them. I know you didn't come all the way over here to talk about what I am wearing to the gym."

"No."

"What the fuck did you come through here in the first place for?"

He stared at her legs then her breasts and she said, "Why are you here?"

"I didn't like the way our last conversation ended."

"What are you talking about?" She walked to the fridge and got a bottle of sparkling water. "Okay, you didn't like how our conversation went?"

"I didn't."

"What didn't you like about it? I mean all I was doing was telling you what was going on. I told you that they were onto you and you show up at my house after I lied to them about you."

"That's not what I am talking about? I am talking about the fact that you sounded like we weren't together anymore."

"Fresh, cut the bullshit. You know we're not together and you know you don't give a fuck about nobody but yourself."

"I love you, Jada."

She turned away. She didn't want to see his face. Didn't want to hear those words. Didn't like the way he toyed with her feelings and emotions. "Look, I'm too grown to be playing these silly-ass games with you, and I find it hard to believe that you love anyone. You are incapable of love."

"It's not true."

He stepped toward her and embraced her. She loved the way he held her. She felt protected in his arms, but she was not about to be a fool for this man. She pushed him away from her and then faced him again. She took a swig from her water. "So you love me?"

"I do."

"Prove it."

"What do you want me to do?"

"Call your baby mama now and tell her that you are in love with me."

A silly-ass grin appeared on his face. "You don't believe I'll call her?"

"No."

He removed his phone, found his baby mama in his contacts, and called her. He ended the call before she answered.

"Get the fuck out!"

 He laughed and said, "Now is the part where you call me a fuck-boy."

 "You know what you are."

 "That's fucked up."

 "What's fucked up is that I lied to them white folks for your ass, for a man that didn't love me, now you can go on. Get the hell out. Right now."

She walked over to the door and opened it. He walked out. When he was on the other side of the door, she said, "I hope you were smart enough to move."

 "I did."

 "Good."

"Do you want to know where I live?"

"For what?"

There was a long pause then he attempted to step back inside her home, but she slammed the door in his face.

 "Fuck-boy!"

CHAPTER 3

An unidentified number called TeTe and she answered on the first ring. "Hello?"

"Hey, Ms. TeTe, this is Casey."

"Who?"

"Casey."

"I don't know no Casey."

"Fy-head."

"Oh hey, baby! How are you doing?"

"Not too good. I just got out and I ain't got a pot to piss in. I hate asking people for money, but I really need your help. Do you have anything for me to do, Ms. TeTe? I ain't even got a place to live. Mama said I can't come to her house, talking about I'm a bad seed."

"I'll text you my address and you can come over later tonight around six o'clock."

"Thanks, baby."

Fy-head and another tranny named Diamond Princess arrived at TeTe's home around six-thirty. TeTe invited Fy-head in and hugged her. Fy-head introduced TeTe to Diamond Princess.

TeTe said, "I'm so glad you out. So what happened with your case?"

"I'm out on bond, but I know I'm going to beat the case, you feel me? That motherfucker tried to choke me and I slit his goddamned throat." Fy-head lied; she had planned to kill Craig all along, but she decided it was best that she told everyone the same story and convince herself that's the way it happened. It was self-defense and her attorneys had told her that they would easily prove it was self-defense because Matthews had killed one tranny and he had had his wife killed.

"I'm so glad you're out."

"Me too."

TeTe looked at Diamond and sized her up. An amazon with a voluptuous backside and TeTe wondered if the tranny wanted to get paid.

TeTe passed Fy-head a thousand dollars.

"What is this for?"

"You just got out."

"I know, but you don't owe me no money, Ms. TeTe. I was wondering if you had anything for me to do. I like to earn my money. I don't want no handouts."

"I can't hire you with your status," TeTe said as she spoke of Fy-head's HIV status.

"I know."

"Well, I do have one job for you to do. It will be just to accompany the girls when they meet these creepy-ass dudes, but you're going to have to get in touch with your masculine side for that. You are going to need to be a boy, understand? I need you for protection."

"Honey, I can do whatever you want," Fy-head said. "Don't get it twisted. I can fight. I'll beat a motherfucker down."

TeTe looked at Diamond Princess and said, "So, you want to get paid or what?"

"Depends."

"First of all, what's your status?"

"I'm negative."

"Perfect."

"I didn't say I was going to do it."

"Yet." TeTe laughed.

Ava and Shamari lay on her sofa inside her loft kissing, "I'm so glad you're here with me."

"Of course, I'm going to be here with you. I'm sorry that shit happened to you."

"I need help."

He untangled her hair with his hand, "I'm here for you, baby. What do you need for me to do?"

"Help me find this motherfucka We got to get him before he get me. I'm scared."

"Hold on a minute. We don't need to find nobody. I got other shit to take care of."

"Like what?"

"Finding out who killed Black."

"Your friend is dead and we can't bring him back. I'm right here with you. You have to help me."

"Nothing is going to happen to you. I can promise you that."

She turned to the side and presented a blackish mark on her stomach right above her belly button. "You see this?"

Shamari stared at the scar on her stomach.

"What is that?"

"This is where I was shot."

"Who shot you?"

"One of Mario's goons."

"Who the fuck is Mario?"

"The guy that I took the money from. His name is Mario and he is the one that shot up my car. Do you even listen to me?"

"I didn't remember the name. Can you please just calm down?"

They exchanged stares.

"So, he shot you or had you shot?" Shamari asked.

"Yes." Ava said. She lied. She had gotten shot by an older sugar daddy that had found out that she had slept with his richer white friend. But Shamari didn't need to know that.

"Okay, I'm not understanding. Why didn't they kill you?"

Ava looked away from Shamari and she gathered her thoughts. The lies she would tell him. "Well, I was at home one night and I heard a loud boom. Before I knew it, there was a man standing over my bed and was pointing a gun at my head. But my dad had just gotten out of jail and he was sleeping over that night. He rushed to my bedroom and wrestled the man, but only after he'd let off a shot. My dad killed the man," Ava said.

"Damn, Shawty."

Ava sighed then said, "I've lived a rough life."

"I see."

"Understand now why you have to help me? We have to kill him before he kills me."

Shamari stood from the bed and slid into a pair of shorts and then said, "Look, I'm not about to go looking for someone that I don't even know to try to kill them. What the hell do I look like?"

"You said that I was your girl. You said that we were going to be together."

Shamari looked at Ava with serious eyes and said, "Look, shawty, I really do care about you, but I don't know you good enough to be going out killing somebody for you."

She stood and approached him then draped her arms around him and lay her head on his chest. She heard his heartbeat. "I don't want them to kill me, Shamari."

"Nobody is going to kill you."

"You don't know that." She released him and began to pace again. "You're not going to help me?"

"I didn't say that I wasn't going to help you. I just said that I'm not looking for someone to kill because you want me to."

"I understand."

"Do you really?"

"I do and I love you."

He kissed her forehead.

* * * * *

31

TeTe called Ava and told her that she had a job for her that was going to pay her twenty grand for one night and it was local.

"I know you said that you were out of the game, but this is a lot of money for one night. He requested you. Also, I have a birthday special going where if a client has a birthday, we are sending two girls for the price of one."

"You know I'm not interested in that. Why would I want to split my money?"

"I'm the one taking the loss for the birthday special and both of the girls will get paid the normal fee.

"How did he request me when I told you two weeks ago that I wasn't going to work anymore?"

"Your picture is still on the website."

"Please take it down."

"The football player requested you again, too."

"Please take my pic off the website."

"All right, all right, I'll take it down, but are you sure you don't want this job. Twenty thousand for one night and I'll give you fifteen of the twenty," TeTe said. "Look, if it's Shamari you're worried about, I won't tell him shit."

"What about Jada?"

"What about her?"

"I can't have you telling that ho nothing either."

"This is just between you and me."

"Give me the details."

“Penthouse suite of the St. Regis. The client is going to leave you a key at the front desk. All you have to do is go to the desk and present your ID and they will give you the key. You take the special elevator to the penthouse.”

“Who is the guest?”

“I don’t have the information in front of me, but if he’s paying that much money, I’m sure he’s some rich, old white dude.”

“When is the gig?”

“Tomorrow night at eight-thirty.”

“I’ll be there.”

TeTe said, “Good and this is just between me and you.”

Ava's instructions were to go to the front desk of the condo building and get the key for room 2105. The concierge was a pretty, tiny black girl named Bethany. Ava asked for the key as she presented her ID. As Bethany handed Ava the key, Bethany said, "I see you like the Spanish Papis too."

"Excuse me?"

"Your man, girl." She winked.

Ava smiled and thought nothing of it until Bethany said, "Just between you and me, one of them tried to hit on me."

"What are you talking about?"

"Yeah, the cute, short one named Chico. Think he said he was from North Carolina somewhere."

"Can you describe the other one? Make sure we are talking about the right people."

Bethany went on to give her a description that seemed like she was describing Mario. Ava left the building thinking it had to be him. Mario, her nemesis from her past, was in Atlanta. And he'd riddled her car with bullets after he had found her. She walked out of the building and called TeTe.

"I have a family emergency and need to travel back to Charlotte. I can't make the date."

TeTe was furious. She hated to disappoint her clients, but she called Willow, her new girl, to take Ava's place.

It was eleven p.m. when Willow arrived at the building. She punched in the access code and took the elevator up to the eighteenth floor. She knocked on the door. A Latin man opened the door and invited her in.

 "Happy birthday," Willow said.

The man said. "It's not my birthday. Why did you think it was my birthday? Close though, my birthday is three weeks away."

"I don't know. This month we're doing a lot of birthday specials where you get two girls for the price of one."

The man looked confused and he said, "Perhaps that explains why you're here then because I asked for Ava. So you're the additional girl?"

There was a knock on the door and he turned to Willow and said, "Excuse me."

"Sure."

He opened the door and there was a statuesque blonde with lips, fillers, and cleavage spilling from her sequined dress, smiling hard with ultra-bleached teeth. She was carrying a three-tiered lemon cake in a box.

"Can I help you?"

"Happy birthday."

"It's not my birthday."

"I'm Nicolette and I was sent to party with you for your birthday."

"Where is Ava?"

Nicolette frowned and said, "I don't know Ava."

"Nicolette, there have been some kind of mix-up. It's not my birthday until later this month."

She frowned and walked away.

He closed the door and Willow said, "Evidently there must have been a mix-up at the agency. Everyone thinks it's your birthday."

"Apparently, but my birthday is three weeks away. Where's Ava?"

"I don't know her, but supposedly she had some kind of family emergency at the last minute. But since it's not your birthday, I'm probably the only girl you'll get." Willow smiled and said, "Take me or leave me?"

Willow looked great. Her hair was in a bun and she wore a yellow dress and heels that accentuated her long legs. She wore a little makeup, and she had a sparkling smile.

"I supposed you can stay," the man said. "What's your name?"

"My name is Willow and what's yours?"

"My name is not important to you."

Willow eyed the man and he was indeed an attractive man wearing a white shirt, tight white jeans and driver shoes as well as a Breitling watch. He had to be rich, perhaps a baseball player. Willow had worked for TeTe for two weeks, and she was happy that she had decided to work for her. She had met so many fascinating clients. There were so many rich men and she'd made so much money. Unlike working from an ad on Backpage where she could sleep with three men and not even make a thousand dollars.

"So your name is not important?"

The fine-ass man ignored her then offered her a drink.

"What do you have?"

"Whatever you want."

"White wine, please."

He disappeared into the kitchen and his ass looked fantastic in those tight white pants. A minute later, he returned with two glasses of Riesling. "You can call me Hector."

"You don't look like a Hector."

"What do I look like?"

"Rico Suave. You're a good-looking man."

"And you're not so bad yourself."

She sipped the Riesling "Thanks. I don't know if that was supposed to be a compliment."

"I've had better."

"Fuck you, asshole." She stood and started walking toward the door. "I didn't come here to be insulted."

The man named Hector said, "I didn't mean it to be offending. All I meant was there is always someone better looking than you and me. There is always room for improvement."

She took her seat. "I guess you're right."

"Of course, I'm right."

"So, if you had to improve me, what would you do? I was thinking about rhinoplasty.

He said, "Absolutely no surgery. I hate surgery. You're natural. You just need to gain about ten pounds and work out a little. Tone that flat ass up."

She smiled. Maybe he wasn't an asshole after all.

He said, "Tell me about Ava."

"I don't know her. Never met her. Why are you so hung up on her?" She removed her iPhone from her purse, went to TeTe's company website, and found a picture of Ava. "She's beautiful."

"Yes. but so are you. I've had better than her too."

"You're so hard to please."

"Actually, I'm not."

There was a knock on the door. Rico Suave answered the door. Two Latin men stood there—a big one and a medium-sized one that had darker skin, but Willow could tell that they were Hispanic, too. Rico Suave stepped out into the hallway and she could hear them argue, but she had no idea what they were arguing about since they were speaking Spanish. A minute later, Rico Suave was back inside. The men had left.

He put on some salsa music and asked if she danced.

"I do dance, and I like salsa but I don't know how to dance to it that well.

"I'll teach you. If you relax."

She smiled. She liked him and he made her feel at ease as she watched his sexy body. He unbuttoned his shirt, revealing very beautiful-looking tanned abs. She'd never had a man that exuded so much sexual energy. She liked him a lot and she wished that she could have a man like this as her boyfriend until he said, "I have a weird request."

She said, "What is it? I've heard it all."

"Are you into prostate play?"

"What's that?"

He smiled and said, "I'm giving you an education. Now I'm telling you what prostate play is."

"Yeah."

"Well, prostate play can enhance a man's orgasm."

"You want me to stick my finger in your ass?" She laughed and she could tell that he was getting annoyed.

"What's so funny?"

"Nothing is funny."

"Something is funny or else you wouldn't be laughing."

"Hey, if you want me to stick my finger in your ass, I'll do that. You're paying good money."

"That's not what I want you to do."

"Well, what is it?"

He went to the bedroom and returned with a huge, black, veiny dildo with a huge head on it.

Her eyes grew. "What do you want me to do with that?"

"I'm not gay."

"I didn't say you were, and if you were, it would be your business." She was thinking that the tight, nut-hugging pants made sense now.

"I want you to fuck me in the ass, but because you're a woman and you fuck me in the ass that means that I'm not gay."

"Okay, we've established that."

Rico Suave removed his pants and revealed some very tight black silk underwear. He pulled them down around his knees. He kneeled over and put his hands on the head of the sofa. She strapped on the dildo and plunged it deep into his asshole. She felt like a butch. She felt frustrated and disgusted. She kept pounded his cheeks as he cried, "Harder. Harder."

* * * * *

TeTe called Ava the next day and asked was everything okay.

"Yes...well, no."

"You want to talk about it?"

"Can I come over?"

"Sure."

Later that evening, Ava visited TeTe's home. They sat at the bar and drank Moscato.

"Look, I'm really sorry about what happened the other night, but I don't know if I told you I was running."

"Yeah, you said from your boyfriend."

"I lied."

TeTe's eyebrows raised. "What do you mean?"

"I'm not running from my boyfriend. I'm running from some D-Boys from North Carolina."

"What happened?"

"I took some money. Lots of money."

"What do you mean lots of money?"

"I stole a million dollars."

"What?"

"Yeah, I was young and stupid and I was listening to my friends and we took a million dollars from a D-Boy and I think they know I'm in Atlanta. The other day, my car got shot up and I'm pretty sure that it was them."

"What did Shamari say?"

"He says nothing is going to happen as long as I am with him, but something did happen and I think they are your clients. That's why I cancelled."

"Who is the guy that tried to kill you?"

"His name is Mario."

"The client's name was Hector Gonzales."

"Look, when I entered the building the other day, I spoke with a woman in the lobby. She was going on and on about how fine Latin men are and asked was I going to the apartment. She said she had met one of the men from the apartment and they had told her that they were from North Carolina. Think about it. I took a million dollars a couple of years ago. My car gets shot up and now, I'm supposed to meet up with some Latin men from North Carolina. Not Miami, Not Atlanta, but North Carolina. It's them, I know it's them."

TeTe said, "There is more than one Hispanic man from North Carolina. Look, I'll ask the girl that I sent how did the man look and then we can compare descriptions."

TeTe telephoned Willow and asked her to come right over while she and Ava enjoyed Moscato and finger sandwiches. Willow came over and pointed to Ava as soon as she saw her and said, "You're the girl."

"What girl?"

Then she glanced at TeTe and said, "She is the girl that my client kept asking about. Kept comparing me to."

Ava said to TeTe, "See, I know what I'm talking about."

"That doesn't mean shit," TeTe said. "You are the one that he requested."

"He wants to kill me."

Willow said, "Oh, no, honey, he didn't want to kill you. If you ask me, he wanted to lick the bottom of your feet."

TeTe poured Willow a glass of Moscato and asked, "What did the guy look like and how was he?"

"The man was beautiful, very attractive. We had a good time but he was weird. His requests were quite weird. I know that I'm going to be asked to do a lot of crazy shit, but this was a bit much."

"Did he ask you to fuck him in the ass with a dildo?"

Willow's eyes lit up. "That's exactly what he asked me to do. How'd you know?"

"Because I think the motherfucka is bisexual. I'm telling you, I think he's gay, but he always have these crazy requests," Ava said. "So what did he tell you his name was?"

 Willow sipped her wine and then said. "He didn't want to tell me his name at first but he eventually said that his name was Hector."

 "Hector?"

 "Yes."

 "That's not his real name. That man's name is Mario. . You didn't happen to take a picture of him?"

Willow started giggling and TeTe asked what the fuck was so funny.

"Actually, I did take a picture. A video I was going to send it to my girlfriend."

"Let me see the video." Ava said.

Willow found the video on her cellphone, then presented it to TeTe and Ava. All they could see was a man's house getting pounded by a big black dildo.

TeTe was annoyed. "Hell, that could be anybody's ass."

"That's Mario's ass." Ava said. "I'm telling you, I used to fuck him all the time."

Willow said, "So this man's name is Mario?"

"Yeah."

"I don't understand. What the hell is going on?"

"He wants me dead. That's what's going on."

"No way," Willow said. "Hector is harmless." She laughed and said, "But there were two shady-ass Latino men that came by the house and they all went out into the hallway."

"That don't mean shit, but if it will make you feel better, I'll get John my P.I. to check into it for you."

"Thanks, TeTe."

Jada was lying in bed about to watch *Power* when her doorbell rang. She made her way to the front door and asked, "Who is it?"

"It's me."

She recognized the voice but couldn't place it. She looked through the peephole and saw that Tank was on the other side of the door. She opened the door and invited him in. She had to admit the motherfucker looked damn good. He was wearing chinos, Adidas mesh shoes, and a nylon shirt. He had grown out a very well-groomed beard.

"What brings you here and who told you that you could just pop up at my house? How would you like it if I popped up at your place? Oh my bad, I forgot, I don't know where you live."

He frowned. "Jada, the comedian."

Jada bit into her sandwich and said, "Would you hurry up. *Power* is about to come on."

"DVR it."

"Good idea." She disappeared into the room and set the DVR and then came back inside, still holding onto her half-eaten sandwich.

Tank was looking at her like he wanted to throw her down on the floor, rip the clothes off her right then and there, and fuck her like an animal.

She bit her sandwich, "I suppose Country has had her baby."

"Who?"

"You know I call your wife Country, stop playing."

He laughed and she had to admit he looked sexy as fuck with his beard. "Jada, Jada, Jada, you always got jokes."

"What do you want with me, Tank?"

"I wanted to see my friend."

"Now you see me, but I know damn well you didn't come here to see me. You got pics of me in your phone I'm sure."

"Look, I want us to get back together."

"Were we together?"

He laughed but didn't answer the question.

"What you mean is you want me to resume my side-bitch duties and you resume your pay-master duties."

"What?"

She finished her sandwich before saying, "Friends with benefits, motherfucka. That's all we ever were—friends with benefits. I made the dumb mistake of liking your ass, but I should have known."

"I like you too, Jada. Why do you think I'm here?"

"Whatever, Tank."

There was an awkward silence and finally she said, "You never answered the question?"

"And what question was that?"

"Did your wife have the baby?"

"No, she has it this month."

"Shouldn't you be home with her?"

"She's fine. Her sister is with her."

Jada rolled her eyes and said, "Old trifling ass."

"I can't help it. I like you."

Jada grabbed Tank by the arm and led him to the door. She stole a look at his ass and thought damn that motherfucker was fine.

Tank turned and faced her when he was outside. He extended his arms and said, "Can I get a hug?"

She said, "I suppose." She leaned into him and hugged him. He grabbed her ass and she didn't move his hands. She loved his cologne "1 Million" by Paco Rabanne.

Jada fixed herself another sandwich and was in bed for ten minutes watching *Power* when she decided to text Tank.

Jada: Damn! I didn't know I missed you so much!

Tank: I know. I missed you too.

Jada: I hate yo ass, but I want you inside of me at the same time.

Tank: Let's make it happen.

Jada: Come over and watch Power with me, ole trifling ass.

Tank: I'm on my way.

As soon as Tank stepped inside, Jada peeled her panties off. Tank kicked his shoes off, scooped her up, and carried her to the bedroom. He laid her on her back. The TV was playing in the background. Jada said, "I thought we were going to watch *Power*?"

"I thought you said you want to feel me inside you?"

"I do."

"We can watch *Power* later."

Jada reached over and took possession of the remote. She ended the TV. Tank came out of his T-shirt and pants and then his socks.

She turned over to the nightstand and opened the drawer. She removed a gold Magnum condom and handed it to him.

"What is this for?"

"Nigga, I ain't trying to get pregnant. I don't know where you been."

His dick was now erect. He ripped the condom packet with his teeth and put the damn thing on backwards. She could tell because the lubrication was on the outside.

She was laughing at his silly ass. Then she handed him another. "Do you want me to put it on for you?"

"No, I got it."

"Ain't used to using them, huh?"

"Whatever." He struggled to place the condom but finally got it on.

She turned on her side and he entered her and spooned her. Even with the condom on, she felt so good to him. She was so tight. He had forgotten what he had been missing. He was looking at her pretty ass and those tits were looking perfect with pretty-ass nipples poking out. She had tried to be hard and she had hung up on him several times during the past couple of weeks, but he knew that if she saw him that she wouldn't be able to resist him. She would bitch about the baby and then ask him was he still married, but he knew that it would ultimately come down to this. He'd have her ass in the air. He knew this because chicks like Jada always wanted a man with money and he had plenty of money. In a weird, sick, kinda way, he knew that she was right. It was a friends with benefits relationship and it aroused him. He felt powerful over the fact that he could get women to fuck him because he had money.

He lay on his back and she hopped on top of him. Her hands pressed his chest as she straddled him. Then she turned around and rode him. His hands were on her pretty ass as she rolled. He came hard inside her.

An hour later, after they showered and they were laying in the bed watching TV, Jada asked, "Did you miss me?"

He sat up on the bed and said, "I did."

"Why did you hurt me?"

"I didn't know I hurt you. Like you said, it was friends with benefits and I was cool with that."

"Were you really cool with that? Because you seemed very jealous every time you sensed I was with someone else."

"I know. I guess we lie to ourselves and say there is no feelings and that this is friends with benefits, but when you really like someone and connect with them, feelings get involved."

"So why did you hurt me?"

"How?"

"The baby."

"She's my wife, Jada. She was my wife before you."

"I know but I…"

"What?"

Jada started crying and he held her and said, "What's wrong?"

She pushed him away. "I guess we can't help who we are attracted to."

"What about the other dude?"

"What other guy? That guy you saw me with last? He was murdered. That was my homeboy."

"Murdered? What happened?"

"Long story."

"I wasn't talking about him anyway. I was actually talking about Fresh."

"He's dead too as far as I'm concerned."

"But you were with him?"

"I wasn't with anyone when you and I were seeing each other. You have a wife and I was just keeping my options open. Men do it all the time."

"I know, but how did I hurt you?"

"Never mind, Tank."

"I want to know."

"You'll never understand."

"I want to be there for you."

"But you'll just leave me in the end."

He held her close and said, "I'll never leave you, Jada."

And in that moment, she felt protected. She felt wanted..

Micky gave Blue a pound when she entered Stunna's home.

Stunna was sitting in the living room drinking cognac straight from the bottle and watching *Outside the Lines*. Micky sat in an armchair across from him. He offered the bottle. She declined.

"What's on your mind?"

"A lot."

Stunna looked stressed and Micky didn't like seeing her brother look this way. He took a sip from the cognac.

"Mick, I was wrong about Goldie and I'm sorry about that. I'll call her personally and tell her that I was wrong, but I wanted to tell you."

"Bruh! It's okay; you were just looking out for me."

Blue entered the room and he sat on the opposite end of the sofa. He dropped a bag on the floor.

Stunna looked at Micky. "Your girl, Kelsey?"

"Yeah?"

"That bitch ain't no good."

Micky frowned. "What?"

"Mick, she's the one that set you up and had those dudes take my work from B.C."

Micky said, "No way. The Feds took that shit from B.C."

Blue dug into the bag he was carrying and removed two badges, One FBI and one DEA.

"What are those?"

"These are the badges the niggas were using to take the work from B.C."

"So you trying to tell me those weren't Feds that took B.C.'s work?"

"No, they weren't."

"How did they know that B.C. had your product on his truck?"

Blue and Stunna looked at each other frustrated. "This is what I'm trying to tell you, Mick. Your girl told them everything and she set you up the night that you got raped."

"She was with me. She was with me and the dude when we got into it in the club."

"Mick, that was all staged. So you wouldn't think that she had anything to do with it."

"And how do you know this?"

"It's amazing what a motherfucker will admit to when you got a pistol in his face."

"So, you caught up with the nigga that actually raped me?"

"No." He paused then took a swig from the bottle and then passed it to Blue. "Remember the fat boy that was at the club the night of the rape? He told me where his cousin lived and his cousin told me that Kelsey and New York set you up. She set you up, Mick, and she took my shit."

Micky stood and was about to leave. Blue had the bottle up to his lips but he quickly grabbed her by the arm and stopped her with his free arm. He set the bottle down and said, "Micky, you know damn well your brother is not going to lie to you."

"Blue, get your goddamned hands off me."

Stunna stood and said, "Let her go, man. Fuck her. I almost got killed last night trying to get to the bottom of this shit and this is how she treat me? Let her go, bruh."

Micky turned and faced Stunna. "What do you mean you almost got killed?"

"I was shot for your stupid ass!"

"You look like you're fine to me."

"I'm fine because I had a vest on."

"Look, bruh, you know I love you, but I don't believe this. You've never liked anybody that I've ever fucked around with and you don't like the fact that I like girls. I know that."

Micky headed toward the door and Blue tried to stop her.

Stunna said, "Let her go."

* * * * *

When Micky entered the house, Kelsey was standing over the stove stirring green beans. She was wearing a lace bra and high rise garter with six inch heels. Micky stared at her. She turned and smiled then attempted to hug Micky, but Micky pushed her away.

Kelsey frowned. "What's wrong?"

"I want to talk."

"Is this serious?"

"Very."

Kelsey turned off the burners on the stove. Mac and Cheese and Potato salad with Cornish hen sat on the counter. They sat at the kitchen table.

Kelsey said, "I don't like the way you are looking at me."

Micky sighed then placed her elbows on the table. "I just left my brother's house and he said that you set me up. Said that you told New York about how he gets product sent and New York took his work from a U.P.S. driver."

"What? I don't even know New York. You need to go talk to your girl Goldie."

"Look, I'm talking to you."

Kelsey frowned and said, "I hope you don't believe this silly-ass shit. I was with you the night you got raped, remember?"

"I know. That's why this whole thing ain't making sense to me."

"It's because it's a lie."

"Why would my brother make this up? He liked you. He didn't like Goldie, but he liked you," Micky said.

"Look, babe! You know I would never do anything like that. I would die for you, babe. I'm the one that saved you."

Micky said, "You saved me by telling him where the work was. The motherfucker still rammed his dick inside of me." Micky covered her head and said, "I don't know what to believe right now. I'm so frustrated."

"Believe that I love you."

"So does my brother."

Kelsey approached Micky's side of the table and put her arms around her. "I'll always be there for you and you'll always be there for me. That's the way it has been."

Micky said, "You know how I feel about my brother."

"And you know how I feel about him. He's my big brother too, but he's wrong."

"Why would he make this up?"

"Who told him this?"

"This guy named Teddy."

"Who is Teddy? I don't know anybody named Teddy."

"Teddy was killed last night."

"Well, Teddy is not here. So how can we prove it?"

"I supposed we can't."

Kelsey kissed Micky and said. "Relax, baby. I want you to go to the bedroom and take a shower. Get into bed. I'm going to finish cooking this meal, and we're going to have mind-blowing sex."

Fresh entered the showroom as Starr and Brooke were rearranging a showcase. Starr turned to Brooke and said, "Excuse me for a moment." She approached Fresh. "So what's going on? What brings you here?"

"Well, I didn't have your number and I was wondering if you could get in touch with Jada for me."

"Follow me to my office."

Fresh was trailing Starr to her office, stealing glances at her ass in her very tight pantsuit. They walked past Brooke who smiled and said hi. Fresh just nodded at the young girl, then the thought popped in his head that Starr's nephew was fucking the hell out of her. When they were in the office, Starr called Jada.

"Hey, girl."

"Somebody wants to talk to you."

"Who?"

"Fresh."

"Who is Fresh? I don't know no Fresh."

Fresh received the phone from Starr's hand. "Jada, I want to talk to you. I'm about to turn myself in and I wanted to see you before I left."

"I don't want to see you, Fresh, but good luck to you. And if you ever need something on your books, shoot me a letter. I'm sure I can put you together a little care package. I mean, it's the least I can do."

"Jada, I need to see you."

"What the fuck do you need to see me for?"

"To tell you goodbye."

"Goodbye, Fresh."

There was silence before Jada said, "I'm waiting on you to say goodbye."

"Goodbye."

Stunna and Shamari met TeTe at STK Atlanta and over steaks and wine. Stunna asked TeTe, "How good is your P.I.?"

"He's the best. He is an ex-cop. I keep him on my side."

"Is he expensive?"

"Not at all. He likes young pussy. Get him young pussy and he'll do what you need him to do."

Stunna swallowed hard. "Ain't the nigga like fifty? Anything is young to him."

TeTe said, "What do you consider young?"

"Me? Maybe twenty-five to thirty-five. I don't fuck with them under twenty-five."

"What about you, Shamari?"

"Yeah, I really ain't into young bitches. I don't usually go under twenty-eight, but I like them close to my age."

"John likes them around eighteen."

"Dirty-ass old man."

They all laughed.

Stunna said, "Look, I need a big time favor."

"Now, I don't know if he's going to do any favors. I mean he likes money, just like the rest of us."

"I'll pay him."

TeTe removed her phone from her purse and called him. She invited John to join them. John came in just when the food arrived. He sat beside Stunna in the cramped-ass booth.

Stunna shook John's hand and said, "I need your help, bruh."

"I'm for hire."

"What's your hourly rate?"

"Since you're a friend, you get TeTe's rate." TeTe smiled and he said, "What can I assist you with? Last time we spoke, you wanted to kill FBI agents."

Stunna laughed. "Not today. I want you to trail this girl."

"Girlfriend? Wife?"

"No, she's my sister's girl."

"Your sister thinks she's cheating?"

"Not at all. But I think she is, but nobody is to know about this but the people at this table."'

"My work is confidential."

Stunna grinned. "I like to hear that."

TeTe bit into her steak and said, "If John can't help you, I'll give you your money back."

"Your sister's girlfriend? What's her name?"

"Her name is Kelsey Long."

"Race?"

"She's black."

"Age and is she originally from Atlanta?"

"She's twenty-five and she's from Valdosta."

John said, "Twenty-five," as he scribbled the information down in his notebook.

"Yeah, I know she's too old for you," Stunna said.

The table burst out laughing.

"So what do you want me to find out?"

She's seeing this dude that goes by the name of New York. I don't know much more than that except the cat is from New York. I want you to follow her. Her address is 3489 Birkdale Lane they just moved to Cobb County; she lives with my sister.

"Anything else?"

TeTe wanted to ask John to research this Mario dude from North Carolina, but she didn't want to say anything in front of Shamari. She wasn't sure how much Ava had told him.

John turned to TeTe, "Anything new?"

"Well, except your girl."

"What girl?"

"The Backpage girl, Willow."

"Oh, yeah? I didn't know she was working for you."

"Yes, she called and she's been doing great."

Stunna interrupted and passed John two thousand dollars and asked, "Do you accept cash?"

John folded the bills and said, "I prefer it. I'll get on this job right away."

* * * * *

Starr and Stunna sat in her car kissing inside the parking deck near her studio.

"I wish we could go back to your place, babe. I want you right now." Starr said.

"What's stopping you?"

"I have to work."

"You don't have to work."

"I have a son, remember?"

He frowned and said, "The thing I love about you, I hate. I like the fact that you are a working woman, but man, do this get in the way of the fun that you and I can have."

She frowned. "I know."

She turned and he embraced her. and she said, "I love it when you hold me. I feel so safe. So protected. And I don't feel like that with nobody but my father."

"Not Trey?"

"Trey is not here."

"Trey was the love of your life though."

"Is that a statement or a question?"

He leaned forward and bit her ear slightly. "Was he the love of your life?"

Silence.

"You don't have to answer that."

She turned and faced him and said. "I'm glad. I enjoy being with you."

"Do you?"

"And I thought about what you had said and you make a lot of sense."

"Don't I always?"

"I guess." She laughed at his confidence.

"But I make a lot of sense about what?"

"I like what I like and it's time for me to quit running from that. I like dudes with an edge to them and I shouldn't try to change what I like."

"You mean that?"

"Yes, but I have to look out for the safety of my child first, so I still want to take this slow."

He smiled. He couldn't believe what she'd just said. They didn't have to make it official right now. He would settle for whatever they had established for the time being.

She kissed him again.

Q was six car lengths away with his nine millimeter cocked. He was fuming. He couldn't believe that Starr had moved on so fast. Future and Snoop's *Homicide* was playing in the background. He wanted to empty the clip on Stunna's ass. There were just two problems. The woman he loved was six inches away, and he was already out on bond awaiting trial.

Starr kissed Stunna one more time before hopping out of the car and the Maserati peeled out of the parking lot.

Q hopped out of his car and ran behind her. "Starr?"

She turned and faced him. "Quentin?"

He was breathing vigorously. She swallowed hard.

A white Ford Fusion pulled onto their level. Starr hoped they would park. She was afraid to be alone with Q. She wasn't sure how much he had seen. The Ford Fusion drove up to the next level of the deck.

"What do you want with me?"

"That's your new man, huh?"

"I don't have to answer that."

"You're right, you don't. I mean, it was obvious. You were kissing the man. Right here in my face."

Starr turned and made her way toward the entrance of the building and Q followed her.

She said, "Quentin, you need to get the hell away from here or else I'm going to call the police."

"This is a public parking garage. I paid my money to park here."

"You're right you can park but don't follow me inside the building."

"You don't own this building. You only own the part where your studio is."

Someone honked a horn and Q and Starr looked back at the same time. The Maserati was back and Stunna bounced from the car with his stainless steel Beretta 9 mm. in his hand. He aimed his weapon at Q. Starr saw what was happening and she stepped in front of Stunna.

"No. No, you can't do this. It's not worth it."

"Get out of my way Starr."

Q stood behind Starr. Stunna was a man with nothing to lose. He would definitely bust a cap in his ass. Damn and he was thinking if he couldn't get back to his car, it would be a shootout in this motherfuckin' parking garage.

Starr walked toward Stunna and said, "Put the gun down. It ain't worth it."

Stunna lowered his gun and said, "Look, motherfucker, you got two minutes to get the fuck away from here."

A security guard named Tammy, a young black girl with a curly weave and a protruding stomach appeared with a walkie-talkie in her hand. "I need you both to get in your cars and leave. I don't give a damn what y'all do to each other when you are away from this property."

Stunna hopped into his car and peeled out. His wheels screeching hard.

Two minutes later, Q left as well.

Starr's heart raced.

John was sipping a latte when Stunna walked into a local coffeehouse in Marietta. All Stunna could think about was this old, creepy motherfucker liking eighteen year olds. Stunna sat across from him and ordered an energy drink.

John said, "I've trailed this girl for three days and I swear most of the time she is with your sister. And sometimes they have another girl with them sporting blond hair and a colossal ass."

"Goldie. She's a stripper."

"I'll keep following her if you want me to, but honestly I don't think she's fucking around. They are with each other all day."

"I just had an idea."

"What?"

Stunna slid him a piece of paper with New York's address. "I need you to find out whose name this place is in."

"I can try."

"That's all I can ask."

"Can I ask you a question, sir?"

"Yes."

"What are you doing this for? Why are you trying to find out who your sister's girlfriend is sleeping with? Why does it matter to you?"

"Beef to settle."

"Is someone going to get killed?"

Stunna just stared at John's cornball ass and wondered why was he asking all these goddamned questions. He remembered TeTe saying that he used to be a cop. As far as Stunna was concerned, once a cop always a cop.

John saw the confusion on Stunna's face and said, "Hey, I was just asking. I mean if someone gets hurt, I want to be able to morally live with myself."

"You can live with yourself fucking eighteen year olds and you're an old man."

"Fifty-five is not old."

"It's old to me."

"Hey, I was just asking."

"Look, do you want to do the job or not?"

"Of course I do. I'll give you a call later tonight."

Stunna shook his hand and left.

John called Stunna later that night.

"Let's meet. Same place."

Stunna was about to go make a delivery to a good customer. He looked at his watch. "I can meet you at nine but I'll have to meet you somewhere in the city."

"Where?"

"Flying Biscuit on Piedmont.

"Ok."

"John, why can't you just tell me what you have found?"

"Look, I asked you earlier what you were going to use the information for and you never answered me. I'm not into talking on phones that might or might not be tapped."

Stunna arrived at the Flying Biscuit just after nine. He spotted John sitting in the back of the restaurant. He sat across from John who was eating shrimp and grits.

"I forgot how much I like this place," John said.

"Yeah, I used to come here a lot myself."

"Well, I ran the address of the place and it came back to Hassan Williams. Then I had a friend of mine run the guy's name. He's twenty-nine, lived most of his life in Maryland, but he was born in New York. New York is an alias."

Stunna laughed and said, "So the motherfucker ain't even from New York?"

"Technically is but he hasn't lived there since he was a kid."

"What else you got?"

John dropped a strip of bacon in his mouth and said, "I drove over to New York's house, and you'll never guess who I saw coming to the house?"

"Kelsey Long."

"You guessed it."

"Her and New York went outside to an outside deck and she fucked him on a deck."

"Did you get proof?"

John passed Stunna his iPhone. "Scroll to the right."

Stunna strolled through three or four pics of Kelsey and New York kissing. Kelsey was sitting on a chair with him. New York's hand was on Kelsey's ass. Then there was a picture of what looked like a flat-chested, sixteen-year-old girl licking a cherry popsicle. He'd scrolled too far. He passed John the phone.

John said, "I'm sorry you had to see the last pic." A creepy-ass grin appeared on his face.

Stunna said, "Can you send me the pictures?"

"Yes. You want the one of the girl eating the popsicle?"

"Hell, no."

"I was just kidding, man."

Stunna thought about Micky and how she was going to take seeing the pictures. Seeing the woman that she loved with someone else. He didn't feel good about the heartache he was sure his sister would feel, but he had to let her know that Kelsey was a piece of shit.

John forwarded Stunna the pics.

Stunna passed John another thousand dollars.

"What is this for? You paid upfront."

"You did a good job."

"Well, I tried my best, sir."

The front desk called Starr and said that Stunna was downstairs and he wanted to see her. She was surprised that he had chosen to just pop up, but when she picked up her phone, she saw that he had called a couple of times. Her phone had been silent.

She smiled when she opened the door and hugged him.

"I just saw that I had missed your calls."

"Yeah, I've been trying for the last couple of hours. I didn't mean to just pop up; especially, since what happened the other day."

"I'm sorry for that. I'd been telling him to leave me alone. I told him to leave me alone."

"I know it looked like you needed help."

"I didn't need for you to pull out a damn gun." She frowned. "You scared the shit out of me."

"I'm sorry about that."

"So what brings you over?"

"I wanted to see you and get a clear understanding about what's going on with this man. I know we have spoken about this before but I want to be clear. I want you to make it clear what are your intentions with him."

"There are no intentions. Me and him are not together."

"But me and you aren't together either."

"We're not."

"So what is it? Why does he think he can just show up at your job? Something isn't adding up."

"He thinks there is a possibility."

"How long did you say that you were with him?"

"Not long, but it seems like a lifetime."

Stunna frowned, "That could be taken for good or bad."

 Starr invited him into the living room. She sat on the love seat and he sat in a recliner opposite her.

"Look, we went through a lot."

"Like what?"

"I was pregnant."

"By him?"

"No, by another man, but while I was with him.

"Whoa!"

"It's not what you think."

Stunna crossed his legs. "Tell me."

"We were on a break and there was this dude that was hitting on me. I swear I never meant for this shit to happen but when I thought Q was sleeping with this other chick, I was weak. I slept with his other guy and Q wanted me to keep the baby."

"He wanted you to keep another man's baby?"

"Yes."

"Bigger man than me."

Starr rolled her eyes at Stunna.

"Hey, I'm just keeping it real. I don't know if I could deal with another man's child."

"Okay, but if you and I get together, you would want me to deal with your children, and I would want you to deal with T.J."

"T.J.'s different. His father ain't around. I just don't want all the drama of dealing with the other man. Not so much the children. See with my baby mamas, I can handle them."

Starr sighed, "So though we were together for a short while, we've been through a lifetime of shit."

"Do you believe that he wanted Trey dead?"

"Yes, he admitted that."

"Do you think he had something to do with Trey's murder?"

"Now that, I don't know. The last time he came over he sounded pretty damn convincing that he didn't do it."

"But you don't know for sure?"

"I don't."

"I need you to tell me that you're not going back to this this man. I know we're not together yet, but I need to know if I'm wasting my time."

"I'm not going back with him. It's over between me and Q."

Stunna stood and began pacing.

Starr said, "Baby, I'm not going to deal with that man."

"I believe you. It's just I got something else on my mind."

"What's troubling you?"

"It's Mick, baby."

"What's wrong with Micky?"

"Micky's girlfriend set her up and was responsible for taking my shit. She's the one that's responsible for my losses."

"How do you know that? What did Micky say?"

"It's a long story. A story that you don't need to know about but basically, a dude that was in on it confessed. And then I had a P.I. trail the girlfriend and she's been fucking around with the dude that raped Mick. I have to kill her."

"What?"

"It's true."

"Damn, babe."

"But that's not the worst part. The worst part is I haven't spoken with Mick in a few days. She don't believe me. Can you believe that shit?"

"You're kidding. Why would you lie? You love her. Did you show her what the P.I. told you?"

"No. I just got the information from him about an hour ago."

"What did he tell you?"

"He showed me pictures. Stunna passed Starr the phone and she looked at the pics of the man and woman making out before arriving at a picture of what looked like an adolescent with pellets on her chest sucking a cherry popsicle.

"What the hell is this?"

"Oh damn, that pervert sent me the pic of the girl anyway." Stunna laughed.

"What the hell are you laughing at? This shit ain't funny."

"The P.I. likes young girls."

"Disgusting motherfucker."

"I know. He must have done that as some kind of joke."

Starr deleted the pic and passed Stunna his phone back.

"You're going to show her the pics?"

"I think that's the only chance that she might believe me."

"She that in love?"

"Mick falls fast."

"I thought she had two girls."

"She does, but I don't think she likes Goldie that much and I thought Goldie had something to do with it. It turns out she's innocent."

"And you accused her of setting Micky up?"

"I did, but I'm going to have to apologize."

"Yeah, do that." Starr hugged Stunna. "Good luck and I'm here if you need me for anything."

"I know you are."

* * * * *

She heard salsa before she reached the door. He was playing Dutty Love by Don Omar. Rico Suave answered the door and invited Willow in. He was wearing tight gray chinos, his shirt was unbuttoned, and she could see a gold chain with the Virgin de Guadalupe on it. Sexy motherfucker, Willow thought. Too bad he had those homosexual tendencies.

"Would you like something to drink?" he asked.

"Rum and Coke, please."

73

Willow watched Rico Suave's sexy ass as he made his way into the kitchen and returned with the drinks.

"So this place isn't yours?"

"No. Airbnb"

"I didn't know Airbnb had places like this," Willow said and sipped her liquor.

"I supposed all kinds of people list their place on Airbnb."

"I suppose," Willow said. "I could never even dream about living in a place like this. Not even renting from Airbnb."

The salsa music was too loud. Willow said, "Do you mind turning the music down?"

Rico Suave stood and she saw his dick imprint through his pants. He turned the volume down—A dial located in the wall. Then he sat down and crossed his legs. He stared at her with a creepy grin.

"Why are you looking at me like that?"

"No reason."

She sipped her drink and smiled and he asked, "How old are you?"

"How old do I look?"

"Nineteen."

She laughed and said, "I'm twenty-two but I used to put in my ads that I was eighteen. You know it's better to be young."

"You are young."

"Not to some of these men out here."

"Those men are child molesters."

"Exactly."

There was an awkward silence as they stared at one another and he said, "So you don't like my music?"

"I love salsa music, but not when I'm trying to get a buzz."

"I see."

"So can I ask you a question?"

"What?"

"Is your real name Mario?"

"No, I told you my name was Hector. Why would you think my name is Mario? Who told you that?"

"Oh, good. I'm happy your name ain't Mario because I like you."

"If my name was Mario, then what?"

"Well, that girl that you were looking for? Ava? You know, the one that didn't show up the last time?"

"Yeah, what about her?"

"Somebody named Mario is out to kill her and she told me to find out if your name was Mario. She was going to send goons to kill you before you get her."

"Oh, really?"

"Yes. She was saying something about how she had taken a million dollars from him when she lived in North Carolina."

"I'm Mario."

"You said weren't Mario."

"I lied."

Willow stood and was walking toward the door, but he cut her off. "Where the fuck do you think that you're going?" he asked.

"Look, I don't want any part of this bullshit. I have enough problems."

Mario brandished a gun and said, "Sit down."

Willow returned to her seat and Mario said, "I have a proposal for you."

"What?"

"I'm going to double what you're getting paid to be here if you help me catch up with Ava."

"How?"

"Become her friend. Find out where she lives and I'll give you even more money."

"I hardly see her. I've only seen her once."

"Look, Willow, I'm going to give you twenty-five thousand dollars. That's enough to pay down on a new trailer."

"Fuck you. Just because I was raised in a trailer park don't make you better than me."

"Now you're getting all emotional. I'm offering you twenty-five thousand dollars cash to find out where this woman lives."

"How do I know that you're going to pay me?"

"Because I'm going to give you half up front." Mario disappeared into the room and returned with twelve thousand, five hundred dollars in cash. He passed it to Willow. She'd never seen that much money in her life. The most money she'd ever seen was three thousand dollars in cash and her dad had it in a tomato can when he was selling meth. Now she had twelve thousand dollars on her own.

"Thank you."

"Deal or no deal?"

"Look, I'll try to find out where she lives."

Mario snatched Willow up by the shirt and said, "You will find out where she lives." Then he turned the salsa music back on.

CHAPTER 8

Stunna said to Micky, "I'm glad you came to meet me."

"Why wouldn't I meet up with you?"

There was silence then he said, "Mick, you know I wouldn't do anything to hurt you."

"I know."

He passed her his cell phone.

Micky swallowed hard. "What is this? What are you showing me?"

"Just look at the phone, Mick. Look at the pictures."

Micky stared at the phone and her face went blank before tears welled in her eyes.

Stunna came around the table and held his sister, her head between her legs sobbing. "I can't believe this is her."

"Look, I'm sorry."

"No, it's okay."

"She has to go, Mick."

Micky's eyes met Stunna's eyes and she said, "Not yet."

"What do you mean, Mick?" You know how I roll. I can't let her get away with this. If word gets out that I'm—"

Micky cut him off. "Word's not going to get out about this."

"Talk to her all you want, but you know what has to happen."

Stunna knew from the look in Micky's face that she was still in love.

"Mick, we gotta do it."

"I know."

"I'm sorry."

"No. I'm sorry, bruh."

He hugged Micky and kissed her on the cheek. When he was gone, Micky started crying again.

When Micky got home that night, Kelsey greeted her with a hug like she always did. They sat down at the table ; *Low Life* by Future played through a Bluetooth speaker. Micky was silent and Kelsey asked, "What is the matter with you?"

"You made me look like a fool. A complete fool," Micky said.

"What do you mean?"

Micky slung the bottle of ketchup and said, "You know, I believed you and I didn't believe my brother. I should have known that he wouldn't lie to me. He wouldn't hurt me like you hurt me. I ain't never been hurt like this before."

Kelsey stood up from the table, her eyes on Micky. She walked seductively to the other side of the table and said, "What the hell are you talking about?"

Micky presented her with the pictures.

Kelsey eyes blinked rapidly as she studied the pictures and said, "So you had me followed?"

"What do you think?"

"I'm sorry you found out about this, but I can explain."

"How can you explain that you were fucking the motherfucker that raped me?" Micky stood with her hands on her waist and said, "Please explain this shit to me."

Kelsey started crying. "Look, you had Goldie and I had nobody and I didn't tell him to rape you. I didn't want him to rape you. I didn't know he was going to rape you. I'm sorry! I really am, Mick. I'm sorry. But you know, sometimes I just want a man inside me and as wonderful as you are to me, there is no feeling like a man being inside me."

"So you're not gay? Cuz you told me that you were gay. Told me that you had only been with one man."

"Look, I'm sorry."

"My brother wants to kill you."

"I know."

Micky shook her head asked, "Was it worth it?"

Kelsey's mood plummeted "I know you're angry with me and you have every right to be, Micky, but I swear to God, I never meant to hurt you and I didn't want you to get hurt."

"Sometimes we get hurt by the people we love and sometimes we have to hurt the people we love."

"Please don't hurt me."

"Why the fuck should I let you live. I'm dying inside."

"You love me and we're going to get married and I want to adopt that little boy that you want."

Micky broke down in tears and said, "I can't deny I love you, but give me a reason to believe that this shit won't happen again.

Well, I know it's not going to happen again because my brother is going to cut me off if I deal with you. I have to give up a relationship with my brother if we stay together."

Kelsey smiled, "I'll call New York right now and tell him that it's just me and you."

"I don't think you're going to be able to reach him."

"I just spoke with him this morning. What do you mean?"

"New York might be in the trunk of Stunna's car right now."

"Don't let them kill me, Micky. Please don't let them kill me. I fucked up. I'm sorry. I didn't know that New York was going to do all of this."

"What do you mean you didn't know he was going to do all of this? You told them about the work didn't you?"

"Don't let them hurt me."

Micky said, "I'm not going to kill you, but we gotta get out of here. We have to go somewhere and hide."

Kelsey rushed to Micky's side and embraced her. "Thank you."

Micky said, "I don't know why I love you, but I do."

* * * * *

Starr hugged Stunna as soon as he walked into the house. He was frowning and she could tell he was upset. They sat down and she offered him a sparkling water. He looked at the bottle before he said, "What the fuck is this?"

She laughed. "It's sparkling water."

"You know I don't drink no uppity shit like that. First I thought you were offering me a bottle of wine." He examined the green bottle.

She laughed and said, "No, it's just water, Stunna. Just water, not poison."

He laughed and then he sat down on an end chair.

Starr sipped her water then asked, "Tell me what's wrong?"

He stood and ran his fingers through his hair and glanced in her direction then sat back down.

She said, "I want you to know that you can tell me anything."

"I know."

"Why don't you tell me then?"

"Because I don't know if you want to know. I don't know if you need to know this."

She laughed, sipped her water then stood approached and hugged him. "I have to be honest. First, I didn't know if I wanted to know. Now, I'm curious. You have to tell me."

"I have to kill Micky's girlfriend."

Starr released him. "Whoa."

"I know." He frowned. "Now you see why I didn't want to tell you?"

"I mean I didn't think that you were going to tell me that you were going to kill somebody."

"Hey, I'm a bad guy. You already know this."

"I know."

"I'd told you she had these dudes take my shit?"

"Yeah, you told me but killing her is not going to bring your shit back. Is that the only option?"

"Yes."

"Are you sure?"

Stunna turned to Starr and stared with serious eyes.

"Are you sure that is the only option?" Starr asked again.

"Yes."

"The coke is gone and what's done is done."

"What are you saying?"

"I'm just saying that you don't have to kill everybody that crosses you. You have to be smart."

"What do you suggest?"

"What did Micky say?"

"Micky knows, but I don't think she believes me. I showed her the pics but Mick loves that girl."

"Maybe you can get her to leave Atlanta. Make her leave. You don't have to kill her. Maybe you can make everyone think that you have killed her, make her leave town."

Stunna sighed and said, "You make a lot of sense. I really don't want to kill the woman anyway. Damn, I'm so happy you're in my life."

She smiled and then he said, "Next thing you're going to have me drinking that ole uppity-ass water."

"It's really not that bad."

CHAPTER 9

Ava said to Shamari, "It was him. I found out it was him."

Her eyes were serious and he said, "What do you mean you found out it was him. Who is him?" Shamari asked.

"Mario."

"Mario?"

"Yes. The guy that I took the million dollars from. He's down here and he's trying to kill me."

Shamari said, "How did you find out?"

"TeTe called me and told that she had a big client for me."

"Oh, so you hoeing again?"

Ava said, "Not at all. Calm down. She said that she had this big client and that the client wanted me. She asked me to go see him and I told her I was through with the game, but she sent another girl in my place to meet up with the guy. The man was Hispanic and he wanted to get fucked in the ass and Mario used to like me to fuck him in the ass."

Shamari covered his ears and said, "Whoa, this is just too much for me to comprehend right now."

"I'm sorry."

"Still, that don't mean that it's him. There's probably a million Spanish dudes that wants to get fucked in the ass."

"From North Carolina?"

"Probably. I don't know."

She wrapped her arms around him and said, "I don't think you understand how serious this shit is."

"Oh, hell yeah. You took a million dollars from somebody."

She released him and said, "I know what I did was wrong and I'll never do nothing like that again. But I need your help, babe."

Shamari looked at her without saying anything.

"I know where he's staying," she said.

"So you know where he's staying. What are you asking me?"

She looked away before resuming eye contact with him again. Then she said, "You said you loved me."

"I do."

"Let's kill him before he kills me, babe."

"I'm not looking for that kind of trouble. What I will do is let you move in with me."

"I'm not living in your sister's house."

"No, I'm moving out in a few days. I'm moving into a house out in Alpharetta and I want you to come with me. Nobody is going to fuck with you as long as you're with me."

She smiled. She was glad to hear what he'd just said and she believed that he would protect her, but she needed more than his word. She wanted Mario dead because she knew what he was capable of. She embraced Shamari again.

He nibbled on her earlobe and said, "So you coming with me?"

"No."

He frowned.

"I need more than your promise that nothing is going to happen to me."

Silence.

"So you are not going to do what I need done?"

"What?"

"I need you to kill this man, Shamari. I know that this ain't your business and I hate dragging you into this, but it's the only way that I'm going to feel safe."

"I can't do that."

She hugged him and then waltzed out of the door of his sister's house. He watched her get into a Lexus rental car and speed off.

Rico Suave was wearing pants that were so tight you could see his thigh print. Along with a silk shirt that was unbuttoned at the top, there was a gold chain resting on chest hairs. He invited her in. Pitbull's song" Fun" played in the background. He offered her a drink and she said she wanted a Sangria. He disappeared into the kitchen and returned with two Sangrias.

He lowered the volume of the music down and said, "I have something to tell you."

"What?" Her eyes grew. "Are you gay?"

"What?" He yelled and then slammed the glass down so hard that it shattered into pieces. "What makes you ask me that? Because I let you fuck me in the ass?"

"No...hmm...yes. I don't know," Willow said. "I didn't mean to upset you, really I didn't."

He paced with those tight-ass pants on. She was thinking that he was, in fact, gay but he was still one sexy specimen of a man.

He sat down and crossed his legs. She loved the black Bally loafers he was wearing. He appeared so sophisticated. Men like him never hung around the trailer park where she'd grown up.

She said, "I'm sorry."

"Forget it."

"Okay, you want to tell me something?"

"Yes."

"What is it?"

"I need your help."

Willow gasped then sipped her drink. She was afraid to ask any questions. She didn't want to piss him off again.

"What do you need my help with?"

"Let me start from the beginning."

She sat waiting and staring.

"I'm not a nice man."

"Okay. So is that what you want to tell me?"

"I don't think you understand."

"I think I do."

"What do you think is going to happen to you if you don't tell me where Ava is?"

"I don't know, I guess I'll have to give your money back, but I've spent a thousand dollars of it."

"Wrong."

Her eyes got big. "I don't know where she is."

"Find her."

"And if I don't?"

"You will."

"If I don't?"

"Can you fly?"

"I don't understand."

He smiled. "Willow, I'm not a nice man."

"I didn't think you were."

"So, if you don't tell me where she is, if you don't agree to go along with my plans, I'll push you off the top of a high rise. And see if you can fly."

"I'm going to do what I can."

Rico Suave smiled a sexy-ass smile then handed Willow an envelope of one hundred dollar bills.

"What is this?"

"The other part of the money. I'm confident that you're going to help me."

Willow stood and was walking toward the door when Rico Suave cut her off. She looked confused.

"Where are you going?"

"I thought we were done."

"Not yet."

She sat back down and he disappeared into the back room and returned with a dildo, the same size as last time but this time it was pink. He tossed it to her and dropped his pants.

* * * * *

Starr was surprised when Shantelle showed up at her studio. She hugged her and said, "Would you like something to drink?"

"What do you have?"

"Bottled water. Tap water, sparkling water, some Gatorade."

"I'll take a Gatorade."

Starr asked Shantelle to follow her to her office and once they were seated, Starr presented her with some lime Gatorade.

"So, what brings you here?"

Shantelle looked around at Starr's office. She was so impressed with Starr. Starr was her age. A young black woman, less accomplished than she was in terms of education, from the hood, and yet Starr ran a successful business, living the life that she felt that she deserved.

Starr again said, "What brings you here?"

"I have a confession. I know that you're going to be pissed and you might not speak to me again. But I have to tell you."

"What is it?"

"I slept with Q."

"I could care less about Q," Starr said, thinking the nerve of this bitch coming into her office to tell her that she'd slept with yet another one of her exes.

"But I slept with him before you got with him."

"Okay, so what is the point of you telling me this? I am so confused."

"I saw you a few months ago out with Q and I figured you were with him and that's when I decided to come forward with the information about Q and Trey because I was jealous that you were happy."

"Doesn't matter why you came forward with the information, as long as it was the truth."

Shantelle gulped down her drink. "That's just it."

"What?"

"I don't know if it's true."

"You lied?"

"No. Me and Q had the conversation, but I don't know if he killed Trey. He wanted to kill Trey, but I don't know if he killed him."

"What?"

"Yes."

"Get out, bitch!"

Shantelle stood and was about to walk out the door when Starr stopped her. "Sit down."

Shantelle sat back down and took another swig of Gatorade.

"So you're saying that you don't know whether Q killed Trey or not?"

"That's what I'm saying."

"Look, I'm sorry for how I reacted."

"I don't blame you. I would have reacted the exact same way."

"I don't understand. There are text messages from a Houston phone number telling her to kill him."

"I don't understand that part either."

"Well, it will be for the courts to decide."

"Starr, I'm sorry, I didn't mean for this to happen, but I didn't think I would like you and when I met you, I found out that you were so cool. I hate this had to happen."

"So, you were jealous of me? Why? Shantelle, you're a beautiful woman with an incredible body. I wish I had the discipline to hit the gym like you. You're gorgeous, sweetheart."

"I guess I was just comparing myself to you. Trey had spoken so highly of you and I knew that you had a studio and your interior design business was booming and you're my age—and all the men want you."

"Men don't know what they want." Starr laughed. "Most of them just want to put it in a hole. They don't care what hole it is."

"Ain't that the truth?"

Starr came from around the desk and hugged Shantelle. "How do you feel about me now?" she asked.

"I feel inspired."

Starr said, "Good, I'm here to help."

Ava was at home reading when her doorbell rang. She hopped up from the sofa and she wondered who was at the door. How did they get into the building? It had to be Mario. She kept a nine millimeter under the pillow. She ran upstairs to get the gun and the doorbell rang again. There was no peephole on the door. She stood on the other side of the door with her weapon cocked. "Who is it?"

"It's me."

"Me, who?"

"It's Dave."

It was Cornball Dave, her client. She opened the door and let him in. "David, how in the hell did you know where I live?"

"I followed you one night."

"What?"

"Yes. I know you probably think I'm a weirdo."

"David, that's stalker-type shit."

"How did you get in the building?"

"Some lady just let me in." Dave was wearing some khaki pants and ugly-ass brown wingtips along with some nerd-ass glasses. Whoever let Cornball Dave in the building had determined that he was a very non-threatening black man.

"I wasn't going to come over, but when I called you, you didn't pick up the phone. I don't know why. Maybe something is wrong with your phone because I keep going straight to voice mail."

Ava had blocked his ass a long time ago. The day after he had proclaimed his love for her.

"Yes, I think there is something wrong with my phone. What do you want?"

"I wanted to let you know that I love you. I want to be with you and I want to marry you. I want you to have my kids."

Ava said, "You told me this already."

"I don't think you understand how much I care for you."

"And I care for you, too."

"Why don't you want to be with me? What's wrong with me?"

"Nothing, David. You're a wonderful man, but—"

"But what?"

"David, I'm not ready to settle down. I'm young. I don't think I'll be ready for marriage for a while."

"I know, but you don't understand. I'll wait and I'll take care of you. I'll put you up in a nicer building than this one. One with a first-class gym and room service and all I want you to do is be faithful to me."

"I'm not ready to be committed to one man."

"Is there someone else?"

Ava thought about Shamari and the way he had been acting lately. She wasn't sure what she should call him. They weren't together.

"Is there someone else? You can tell me," Dave said again.

"No. There is nobody else."

His eyes were misty. She felt sorry for him. She opened the door and told him that he had to go.

Micky and Kelsey had traveled to Hilton Head, South Carolina. They rented an oceanfront condo from Airbnb. As they set their belongings down, Micky lay across the king-sized bed inside the bedroom. Kelsey came into the room and lay beside her.

Kelsey looked into Micky's eyes and said, "I'm so happy that you decided not to give up on me, but did we have to go so far?"

Micky looked her in the eyes and said, "My brother will kill you. He was going to kill you. He's probably looking for your little boyfriend right now to get him."

"Don't say that."

"It's true. We are serious about money." Micky stood from the bed and pulled the drapes back to get a good view on the ocean. A storm was on the way and the clouds were low. She was happy because they had been on the road for four hours and she was tired. She wanted to get some rest and she always slept well when it rained.

Lightning crackled as Micky turned to face Kelsey. "I was just thinking about something. You were just defending this New York dude, saying that you don't want my brother to kill him."

"I don't want anyone to die."

Micky stared at her, "I can't believe you let that man rape me. You was in on it."

"Look, I didn't want him to rape you. I swear to God, Mick." Kelsey stood and dug into her bag and found a white Styrofoam box with some zucchini spaghetti and a chicken breast. They had stopped at a restaurant that sold food by the pound and she had stocked up on four pounds of food. "Are you hungry, baby?"

"I don't eat no shit from the side of the road."

Kelsey laughed and then said, "That was not the side of the road. You're always so dramatic."

"Not dramatic, I'm just not eating that garbage."

"Okay, Mick."

"You love him, don't you?"

Kelsey looked confused, but she wasn't confused. She knew exactly what Micky was asking.

"Do you love him?"

Kelsey sat the box down and approached Micky then embraced her. "No, I love you, Mick. I told you the only reason I dealt with him is because you still had Goldie."

"Bullshit."

"I don't want to argue with you."

"Good because my goddamned head hurts. I'm going to lay down and get me some rest."

"I'll pick you up a bottle of Motrin from CVS."

"Okay."

* * * * *

Stunna met with John at a Waffle House in College Park. Neither man ate, but they both had ice water.

"So, what's up?"

"Look, I need help finding my sister."

John took a sip of his water. "When was the last time you seen her?"

"I saw her the night that you had given me the information I needed."

John removed a yellow notebook from a briefcase and said, "I need her name, birthday, height, and last address."

"Can you find her?" Stunna asked as he scribbled the information on to the legal pad.

"I don't know."

John downed his water and called the waitress named Pam over. He asked for more water.

Pam, who held a pitcher in her hand, snarled and said, "This water is for paying customers."

Stunna removed a fifty-dollar bill from his pocket and said, "Apologize, and this is yours."

Pam grinned and said, "I'm sorry."

Stunna said, "You're damn sure sorry, white trash." Then he flagged the manager over and ordered pecan waffles and bacon. He would take the food and give it to the homeless in downtown Atlanta.

John said, "So what happened after I gave you the info?"

"I presented it to her and she didn't believe it."

"You know, I've been a P.I. for many years and I've had men hire me to follow their wives to find out if they are cheating. And after discovering that they were in fact cheating, when I presented them with the evidence, I've seen grown men cry and refuse to look at the pictures."

"Wow."

"Yeah." John stood and then tucked the legal pad into his briefcase and said, "I'll be in touch."

Q received a call from the concierge and they'd informed him that he had a visitor. He told them to send her right up. Seconds later, he opened the door and saw Starr. He looked at her for a few moments. She was smiling and the plunging nude colored V neck dress she was wearing was exhilarating. He invited her in.

There was an awkward silence before he said, "So what brings you here?"

"I received some information today."

He raised his eyebrow "Information?"

"Yes."

"What kind of information?"

"I spoke to Shantelle."

"What did she want?"

"She came over and just basically admitted that she had lied on you."

"I told you that."

"I know and I should have believed you."

"Starr, I told you that I wanted Trey dead, but it was part of the game. I thought he told…"

She cut him off. "You don't have to say a word about that."

"So is that guy your new boyfriend?"

"What guy?"

"The nigga that pulled the gun out on me the other day."

She turned her back on him. Though Stunna was not her man, she didn't want to answer that.

"It's okay, you thought that I was going to go to prison and you moved on."

She turned and faced him. "I didn't move on, we're not together."

"But you like him, right?"

"I do."

"Okay, I wish you the best."

Micky wore a wifebeater, cargo shorts, and flip-flops as she strolled the beach. She'd left Kelsey in the room sleeping. They had been in the South for three days and all the woman did was sleep. Stunna had called her repeatedly. She had sent him to voicemail each time. She had hated to do that to her brother but she knew he wanted to murder Kelsey but she couldn't let him do it. She loved her. Her phone rang; it was Goldie. She answered on the first ring.

"Hello?"

"Bae. I miss you. Where are you?"

"I can't tell you."

"You're with Kelsey?"

Silence.

"You don't have to tell me. I'm not stupid. You know what upsets me the most is that everybody thought I was the gold digger. Everybody thought I was the one that was out for the money because I'm a dancer. But I've earned every dollar that I've ever made. You didn't do shit for me."

"Look, I never thought you were out for my money."

"Why are you with her? You know she set you up."

"What?"

"You think I don't know? Everybody is saying that Stunna is going to kill her and her little boyfriend New York as soon as he gets the drop on 'em."

"Have you seen Stunna?"

"Last night he came by the club and apologized to me and he was asking about you. He's worried about you, Mick! Why don't you answer the phone for him? You know your brother loves you."

The sound of a nearby jet ski whizzing through the ocean drowned the phone out. Micky thought about Stunna. He was all she had and he was doing his best to do what he had always done. Defend his little sister.

"Micky, are you still there?"

"Yes."

"Come back to Atlanta, Micky."

"What makes you think I'm not in Atlanta?"

"I know you, Mick. If you were in Atlanta, you would see me."

A group of teens nearby was screaming, playing volleyball.

Goldie said, "Sounds like you're at the park."

"Look, I gotta go."

"Text your brother and tell him that you are okay."

"You do it."

"I will, but it will be better if you do it."

"Okay, I'll do it."

Micky ended the call and Stunna called. Micky answered the phone.

"Damn, girl, you don't know how to answer the phone?"

"Look, I was just about to call you. I was talking to Goldie and she told me that you had been looking for me."

"You know I've been looking for you, Mick. Don't play dumb. I know damn well you've seen my calls."

"I was going to call you back."

"Why didn't you?"

"Bruh! I can't let you kill her."

"I'm not."

"What?"

"I talked to Starr and she suggested that I just tell her to skip town."

Those damn jet skis were drowning out the phone again.

Stunna said, "Where are you, Mick? And what is that noise in the background?"

"I'm at the beach in Jacksonville." Micky said. She knew Stunna was smart and would probably figure out she was at a beach. But there was no way that she would tell him that she was at a beach in South Carolina.

"She with you?"

Silence. Then there was screaming from the volleyball game.

"That means yes?"

"She's with me."

"Come on back home and just let her stay where the fuck she is, Mick."

"I can't."

"I miss you."

"I miss you too, bruh."

"I love you."

"You know I love you, bruh."

"Come home and help me run the business, Mick. There are a million women in Atlanta and you have Goldie."

"Goldie said that word in the street was that you were looking to kill Kelsey."

"Mick, don't talk like that over the phone."

"So it's true?"

"Why don't you just come home and leave her there?"

* * * * *

Tank, naked with a white towel draped around his ass, was staring inside of Jada's fridge. Scanning the contents, his eyes

105

landed on a container of strawberry Greek yogurt. Then the doorbell rang and he yelled, "Bae, somebody is at your door."

Jada was looking for her phone to open the app to see who was at the door. She couldn't find her phone. She must have left it in the car when she went for a run this morning. She made her way to the door and peered through the peephole before hearing a voice say, "It's me, babe. It's Fresh."

Tank raised his eyebrows and Jada ordered Tank not to move and to stay in the kitchen.

Jada barely opened the door. Fresh stood outside, his hands inside his jean pockets. "You're going to let me in?"

"No, Fresh. You need to leave right now."

"Why?"

"I have company."

"A guy?"

"What do you think?"

"We move on fast."

"So do you."

"What is that supposed to mean?"

Tank tiptoed behind Jada and grinned at Fresh. "You need to leave, bruh."

Fresh saw Tank standing there with a towel around his ass. Clearly they had made love. This infuriated Fresh.

"So it's this clown again."

"Bruh, you need to leave." Tank ate a spoonful of yogurt then he said, "Damn, you were right, babe. This yogurt ain't that bad at all." Then he looked at Fresh. "Did you buy this, bruh?"

Fresh pushed Jada out of the way and removed his gun from his pants pockets. Tank laughed and ate his yogurt.

Fresh pointed the gun at Tank's chest.

"So what you going to do, bitch boy? Shoot me?"

Fresh cocked the hammer.

Jada sprang from the floor and tried to wrestle the gun from Fresh and Fresh slung her ass to the floor. He stepped forward and slapped the fuck out of Tank with the gun. Tank dropped the yogurt, and it splattered all over the floor. Tank was holding his jaw.

Fresh stood over him and pistol-whipped the fuck out of Tank. Blood leaked from his head and mouth as he lay on the floor.

Jada said, "I'm calling the police."

Tank said, "Please, Jada, don't call the police. It's all right."

Fresh pushed Jada out of the way and as he was heading to the door, he turned and said, "This shit is your fault."

Tank stood up and Jada helped him into the bathroom, leaving a bloody trail behind them. She'd cleaned up the gash with peroxide and bandaged him up as Tank sat on the edge of the bed and said, "I'm going to get that motherfucker if it's the last thing I do. I swear to God, Jada, Fresh has to go."

Starr called Stunna over to the studio. He went to the back room with her. When they were seated, he said, "I'm glad you called because I wanted to tell you that I'm going out of town for a few days."

She raised her eyebrows. "Where are you going?"

"South Carolina."

"What's in South Carolina?"

"Micky is there with Kelsey."

"Be careful in South Carolina. Those laws are archaic. North Carolina is okay, but they will hang yo black ass in South Carolina. So you don't need to get in trouble there."

He laughed. "I don't plan on getting in trouble."

"Nobody ever does."

"So why did you call me here? What's up?"

She stood, cut her eyes at him then turned away.

He said, "What's wrong?"

"I have something to tell you."

"Well, that's obvious."

"Look, you're not making this easy."

"Say what you gotta say. I'm a big boy."

Silence. She couldn't look at him.

"Is it about Q?"

"Yes."

"What about him? You about to fuck with him again?"

"No."

"What is it, Starr? I'm a grown-ass man. I don't have time for these kiddy-ass games."

"Look, I found out that he didn't kill Trey."

"Okay. So does that mean you're going back with him?"

"No. I didn't say that. I don't know."

Stunna stood and said, "You know what, Starr? You do what you think you need to do." He tried to walk out of the office but she blocked the door.

"Don't go."

"You want him?"

"I want you."

"So, are we together or no?"

"I don't know."

He moved her away from the door and she grabbed him around his waist, pulling him, refusing to let him go.

He turned and faced her. "I have to go."

She leaned into him and kissed him. His hands cupped her ass and then he yanked those pants down exposing her pretty brown ass in a pink thong. She removed her blouse. Then off came the thong.

"What about Brooke? She will hear us," he said.

"I don't give a damn. I'm the boss."

He dropped his boxers and his penis was fully erect. It was huge. Bigger than Trey's and bigger than Q's; chocolate with a pink head slightly pointing left.

She took him inside her mouth and fondled his balls at the same time. His hand was behind her head forcing his tool to the back of her throat. Her saliva dripped all over his shaft. He felt himself about to cum and he picked her up and sat her naked ass on top of the desk, knocking over some invoices and other important paperwork.

She turned her ass facing him and he stood and plunged deep inside of her wetness as he yanked her hair.

"Yes. I want you deeper inside me. Keep going."

DeSean Cummings had called the agency and asked if Ava was available. He also wanted another girl and TeTe decided that she would send Willow, the new girl. They were to meet at the Four Seasons hotel at 8:30 p.m. Willow was happy to be working with Ava because now she could call Rico Suave and tell him where they would be. She could finally get the other part of the money. He picked up on the first ring.

"Hey."

"Where are you?"

"I'm home."

"What have you heard?"

"I'm supposed to work with her tonight. We will be at the Four Seasons Hotel. I will call you when we're about to leave and I'll

give you the information that you need, like her car. And I'll see if I
can get her to tell me where she lives."

"Perfect."

She hung the phone up.

 Rico Suave paced and clasped his fingers. This was the best news
that he had received in his two weeks of being in Atlanta. He was
finally going to settle the score with Ava. The million-dollar debt
would be paid. He was going to torture that bitch. He'd had
dreams of waterboarding her. Burning her with hot irons. Starving
her for weeks at a time. Making her sleep in a room full of feces
and finally killing her ass.

**Later that night, Ava and Willow met in the lobby of the Four
Seasons.**

Willow said, "So, do you have the key to the room?"

"Yes." Ava gave her a once over. She wasn't a bad looking girl. She
just had the body of a boy. Ava guessed that she would fill out
with time. She and Willow took the elevator up to the penthouse.

"Penthouse suite. This is big time," Willow said.

 Ava just stared at the young girl that was so easily impressed, so
naïve, so gullible. Ava had to remind herself that TeTe had said she
was born in a trailer park. They entered the penthouse.

Willow said, "Wow," as she looked around before taking a seat
and taking a selfie in front of the floor to ceiling glass window. She
would post it on Instagram later. Willow smiled hard as hell as she
walked around looking at the retro furniture, the plush round bed,
and the astonishing artwork. A tray of a dozen chocolate cupcakes
decorated with happy birthday balloons sat on a table that was

located in the center of the room. TeTe had had the cupcakes delivered before they had arrived.

"I love going to these five-star hotels. This is what I like most about this job."

Ava looked at her and rolled her eyes, but Willow didn't notice.

As she lay across the huge bed with her hands stretched out, Willow said, "Can you take a picture of me lying on the bed?"

Ava snapped the picture of the chick and then passed the camera back to her.

Willow stood and texted Rico Suave: *I'm here. She's here.*

R.S: *Perfect.*

Willow sat down at the desk and she started to add filters to her pictures. She said, "Forgive me if I seem like I'm not used to high-class living, but I'm really not."

Ava didn't respond.

"I don't know if TeTe told you, but I was working from Backpage, making 'bout a thousand dollars a day seeing about four to five men a day."

"I would never do that."

"I had to do what I had to do to make ends meet."

Ava looked at her watch. DeSean was already fifteen minutes late. She walked to the window and looked out into the Atlanta night. It had been two days since she'd spoken with Shamari and she wondered what he was doing. She texted him: *Hey, stranger.*

Five minutes had gone by before she realized that he was probably not going to text her back. Silly-ass Willow was busy on social media, snap chatting and texting, when the door opened and DeSean walked in wearing a fitted blue blazer, jeans, and a white Mesh Nikes.

Ava hugged him. "Hey, how are you feeling, birthday boy." She pinched his cheek.

"Better than last time."

Ava introduced DeSean to Willow. Willow shook his hand and said, "You're famous. You play basketball, right?"

"Football. Well, I used to play football. I haven't been picked up by a team."

Willow said, "I knew you were somebody famous."

DeSean was smiling at Willow. "Shorty, you have a pretty face."

Ava was getting kind of mad at him. Damn athletes always wanted some biracial or exotic girl. Plain old black girls wouldn't do any more. But she remembered that he had chosen her off the website. Perhaps he was one of those men that didn't have a type. He never wanted to have sex anyway.

Willow stood smiling at the compliment that Desean had given her.

DeSean said to Ava, "Let's have a party." Then he dug into his bag and removed bottles of Louis XIII cognac that cost $2500 a pop. "So what kind of music do you have on your phone?"

Ava said, "TI, Gucci Mane, Future, Drake, ASAP Rocky, and Yo Gotti. YG, Big Krit, Kevin Gates. You know, the usual."

"What do you have?" he asked Willow.

"21 Pilots, Blink 182, Greenday, lots of alternative stuff. Jay-Z though and Beyoncé."

DeSean said, "Who the fuck is 21 Pilots?"

Willow said, "So tell us what you got on your playlist?"

"I got the same thing as Ava."

Willow said, "I'm confused."

"I wanted to know what everybody had on their play list because I want to have a party. I want y'all to dance for me."

"Like strip?"

"Like shake that ass."

DeSean lifted Willow's blouse and frowned, disappointed in her tiny ass breasts.

Ava said, "I can't dance and it's clear Willow can't dance to trap music either."

"I'm still going to need you to strip down and walk 'round naked anyway."

The girls removed their clothes and DeSean connected his phone to a Bluetooth speaker. Drake's *Child's Play* was blasting through the speaker.

DeSean removed an eight ball of cocaine from his pants and dumped it on a plate. He snorted a line then he asked Willow if she indulged.

"Sometimes."

He dropped his pants and then this underwear. Surprisingly for a cokehead, his dick was stiff at attention. He dumped a line of coke on the shaft of his dick and passed Willow the straw. She snorted the coke off his dick.

Ava was standing there watching this shit. She said, "What the fuck?"

DeSean said, "We're partying, baby. Can you twerk?"

"I can't twerk."

"Party pooper."

Ava folded her arms and DeSean rammed his dick into Willow's throat. She choked and he laughed. He grabbed her by her ponytail and kept ramming it in until she gagged and he let her go. Ava had never seen him act like this.

"What's wrong with you?" Ava asked.

"Nothing is wrong. We're partying, baby."

Ava said to Willow, "Are you okay?"

"Yes, don't worry about me. I'm good."

Willow's phone rang and Ava looked at it.

Ava said, "Your phone is ringing. Somebody named R.S."

"I'll call him back later. It's my uncle."

DeSean downed his bottle of Louis XIII and then passed it to Ava. "Now, I know you're going to drink. It's my birthday."

Ava frowned and said, "I'm not drinking and I don't believe it's your birthday."

Willow wrestled the bottle from her hand and gulped down more liquor.

The phone was ringing. It was R.S. again.

Willow thought she better take the call. She looked at DeSean and said, "I have to take the call. It's my uncle. It may be concerning my granddaddy."

"Take the call, shorty. I'll have more party favors when you come back."

Willow answered the phone and stepped into the bathroom. She turned on the water in the sink to drown out her conversation.

"Where the fuck are you? It sounds like you are at a party and not doing what the fuck I asked you to do."

"I'm doing exactly what you asked."

"What was all the music in the background?"

"I'm with a client."

"With music?"

"Did you forget that I salsa danced with your ass all night? Sometimes clients want to dance."

"Okay, what's going on?"

"Nothing."

"Where is Ava?"

"She is in the room."

"Ok, what time is this little rendezvous going to be over? And you still haven't told me what she's driving."

"I don't know what she's driving. I think this is going to be an all-nighter. It's the client's birthday or he says it's his birthday."

"Text me the address of the hotel."

"Why? Because you can't come up here and kill her. Are you crazy?"

"I'll find it myself. You said you were at the Four Seasons?"

"I will text you when we are about to leave. I'll find out what she is driving."

"Okay. Make sure you call me back."

"Will do."

Willow staggered back into the room and she spotted keys on the dresser and said, "Oh, you drive a Lexus, Ava?"

"No, I've rented one."

"What kind did you rent?"

"Lexus GX460."

"I think I saw a white one out there. Was that yours?"

"No, I'm in a silver one."

DeSean said, "What the fuck is this? Car and driver? We're here to party, not talk about cars."

Ava said, "Not everybody can drive a Rolls Royce like your ass."

"How do you know I got a Rolls?"

"I was just guessing. Am I right?"

"Actually, I have two of them."

DeSean dumped more coke on his tip of his penis.

Willow said, "I bet neither one of y'all know what they call coke on the tip of a penis."

"What?"

"Sheenis. Charlie Sheen used to do this and he had his whores snort it off."

"Sheenis." Ava frowned, "You're such a white girl. I like you though," Ava said, though she thought Willow was a certified cornball.

DeSean said, "Yeah, she's mad cool."

The phone rang and DeSean said, "Tell whoever the fuck that is that it's my birthday. Either they can come over and party or quit calling every five goddamned minutes."

Her phone read missed call from R.S.

He called two more times back to back. She stepped out into the hallway and answered the phone. Wicked by Future was playing in the background.

Rico Suave said, "I have decided to come. I'm on my way to the hotel. Where are you?"

"I've told you where I'm at."

"What is the address?"

"Look, I think it will be a bad idea if you came right now," Willow said, knowing that if he came that even if they didn't kill Ava, she would know that Willow was the one that tipped them off to her whereabouts.

"Look, I will find the place with or without you."

"Find it without me then. Google it."

"I'll kill you."

Willow terminated the call and entered the suite.

Ava was alone and DeSean had gone to the bathroom. Willow just looked at Ava and remembered a few minutes before she had gone out into the hallway how Ava had said that she liked her. She began to feel guilty that she was a part of Rico Suave's scheme. She liked Ava too.

Ava said, "So you're having fun?"

Willow smiled. Ava removed a powder speckle from the tip of Willow's nose

"I am having fun."

"And how old are you again?"

"Old enough."

"I'm just saying you shouldn't be doing these hard drugs. They'll catch up with you in the end."

"Look, my mom was an addict and it's in the cards for me. I have an addict's genes."

"In your case, it's a choice."

"It's not a choice."

"You chose to put that stuff in your nose."

"Hey, we're partying, don't blow my high."

The toilet flushed three times and Ava said, "DeSean, you okay in there?"

"Yeah, I'm taking a shit. Can't a man take a shit in peace?"

The girls giggled.

"Look, Willow, I know I'm not your mother."

"Well, quit acting like it. Nobody can tell me what to do. I've been basically on my own all my life."

"Okay, I'm done with it."

Willow sat on the bed and she stared at Ava and said, "Look, I'm sorry."

"It's okay."

"No, seriously, I'm sorry."

"It is okay."

The toilet flushed six times then they heard the sink running and DeSean was singing along to Desiigner's *Timmy Turner*.

Willow said, "Will you hurry, man? I gotta pee."

The phone rang. It was Rico Suave again.

She stepped into the hallway, rocking side to side, trying her best to hold her pee.

"What do you want?"

"I'm thirty-five minutes away."

"Okay."

"Where is Ava?"

"Where do you think she is?" Willow was being sarcastic.

"If you talk to me like that again, I'll murder your whole family."

"Fuck you, Rico Suave!"

"Who?"

"Mario or whatever the fuck your name is."

"Have you been drinking?"

"I'm wasted and what the fuck are you going to do about it?"

"If you ruin my plans, I'll kill you. I swear."

Willow stepped inside. The water was still running in the bathroom. The door was locked. Trap Music played in the background but DeSean wasn't singing along.

Willow banged on the door. "I gotta pee, bro."

No answer.

Willow banged again. Then turned the knob—locked. She banged harder.

Ava was standing behind her now. Ava pushed her out of the way and began to bang again.

Willow said, "Something is wrong. I can just feel it. Call the front desk."

"Not yet."

Ava removed a pocketknife and attempted to pry open the door. She banged on the door again and shouted, "DeSean, quit playing. Open this damn door."

Willow searched her bag before finding a pair of grey gym shorts and a T-shirt. She threw them on and stepped outside where she spotted a utility worker. A tall, slinky black dude with a greying goatee and a Jesus cross made of red yarn. The utility worker was pushing a cart with a drill, a saw, a hammer, and sixteen different screwdrivers. He was listening to *Victory* by Yolanda Adams on an old school CD player.

She said, "Sir, I need your help."

The grinning-ass slinky dude rushed right over to help pretty-ass Willow. Slinky dude's name tag read "David."

"My friend has locked himself in the bathroom and he's not responding."

The man said, "Where?"

"Follow me."

The man tagged along. He gazed at Willow's tiny ass then said, "Forgive me, Lord." quietly to himself. When they were inside the suite, they found Ava still banging on the door.

David removed a tool from his tool belt and pried the door open. They all rushed inside to find DeSean slumped over the toilet, passed out. David took his pulse.

"Nothing. He's dead." He removed his walkie-talkie from his belt and radioed security, informing them that they had a guest down and to call an ambulance.

David looked closely and realized that he recognized him. "This is DeSean Cummings, the football player."

"No, it's not." Ava lied.

"Who is he then?"

"We don't know," Willow said.

David's mouth flew open then he removed DeSean's wallet from his person and opened it. "It is DeSean. And it says that today he turned twenty-seven years old. What a shame."

Security burst into the room. Two goofy-ass white guys and a black woman with a big butt bursting the seams out of some tight blue security pants. She was fidgeting with a walkie-talkie speaking in some kind of security jargon.

Willow's phone rang. She answered it and stepped outside.

"I'm in the lobby. What floor are you on?

You don't want to come up here right now."

"How in the fuck are you going to tell me where to come? What floor are you on?"

"The police and the ambulance is on the way. The client just OD'd on pain pills."

"What floor? I don't believe you."

"Penthouse, but I'm telling you. Security is on the floor and everything."

Mario and two goons approached the concierge to ask where the elevator was. The man pointed them in the direction of the elevator just as an ambulance pulled up and the police ran into the lobby. The EMTs were carrying a stretcher.

Mario told his goons to hold up.

He called Willow and said, "What the fuck is going on?"

"I'm telling you; the client OD'd."

"Where the fuck is Ava?"

"She is here with me, and we're probably going to have to answer a lot of questions."

"Okay. Call me when the police are done with you."

"Okay."

* * * * *

The concierge informed Starr that Q was downstairs and she asked them to send him up. Seconds later, she invited him in.

When T.J. saw him, he ran and hugged him. "Uncle Q, I missed you."

Starr couldn't help but feel a bit emotional when she saw how much T.J. loved Q.

"Have you been protecting mommy?" Q asked.

"Of course. And Mommy let me play T-ball this summer and sent me to a STEM camp."

What is a stem camp?"

"Science Technology Math."

"Oh wow, you must be smart."

"I always make A's."

Q removed a wad of money and peeled off a hundred. He gave it to the boy.

"I'm going to put this in my bank account," T.J. said.

"You have a bank account?"

"Yes and I have two thousand dollars in it."

"No, you have eighteen hundred in it. Remember, you bought those two games?"

"Oh yeah, I forgot about that."

Starr said to T.J., "Go to your room and play for a minute. Let me talk to Uncle Q."

He disappeared into the room.

"So, what is going on? I know you got another guy. I'm not going to go into it, but it's obvious you like the man. I just need to know if there is a chance for me and you."

"I don't know."

"Yes or no. I'm a big boy."

Starr turned and said, "You know I care about you. But—"

"There is no but. I didn't kill Trey and now you know this. I love T.J. and he loves me."

"Look, Q, I didn't mean to have feelings for Stunna."

"Who?"

"His name is Stunna."

"The very type of dude you don't want me to be." Q laughed.

"It just happened. I mean everything. I thought that you were going down for Trey's murder."

"And you didn't believe me."

"I didn't."

"Is he your man?"

"No."

"Well, then there is still a chance."

She really liked Stunna but she didn't want to hurt Q's feelings and she didn't want to lead him on.

"I swear, Starr, I thought so much more of you than this."

"What is that supposed to mean?"

"You move on really fast."

"I just want somebody to love me. Isn't that what we all want? I want unconditional love. Like my son, he loves me no matter what."

"And so do I. No matter what. You can go out and get pregnant by another man and I still love you. Do you think Stunna would have done that?"

"I don't know." Starr said, but she did know. Stunna had told her that if that situation had happened with him, there was no way he was going to take care of another man's child.

Q leaned forward and hugged her. "I love you, Starr." He walked out the door.

Starr folded her arms and fell to the floor. She realized that she was in love with two men.

Stunna and Blue had received information on the whereabouts of New York. He followed him to the Follies strip club and paid the parking attendant a thousand dollars to turn his head as he abducted New York when New York attempted to get into his Range Rover. Blue and Stunna picked him up and threw his ass in the back of a silver sprinter van and they drove for hours to Hilton Head. It was eleven p.m. when they checked into a Motel 6. Stunna requested a room on the back side of the motel, so they could walk New York's ass up to the room without anyone seeing them. The next day, Stunna called Micky.

"Hello?" Micky said.

"Hey, come to Motel 6. It's right across from where you are staying."

"How do you know where I'm staying?"

"I know everything."

Micky looked at her watch and then stared at Kelsey, who was preparing wheat spaghetti with ground beef. "Look, I'm going to the grocery store to get some milk. Do you want something?"

"No, I'm good."

Micky used her GPS to find out where Stunna was staying and she arrived there in five minutes.

She tapped on the door and when she walked in, she saw New York sitting in the middle of the floor gagged and bound.

Micky walked over and slapped the fuck out of him. Then she spat on him.

Micky said, "Give me a gun and let me kill this motherfucker."

"No, not yet."

"What did you bring him here for?"

The gag had come out of his mouth.

Stunna said, "I don't want to kill him yet."

"Why?"

"I want to kill her."

"I'll take care of that."

"You know, I don't believe you."

"Look, I'm going to do it."

"He was fucking her."

"I know. She admitted it."

"She's pregnant."

"What?"

"Yeah."

"How do you know that?"

"My P.I. followed her to an abortion clinic, but she came out. She didn't go through with the abortion."

"Maybe she did."

"Maybe she didn't."

Blue passed her New York's phone. "Read this text exchange."

New York: I don't want you to kill my baby.

Kelsey: It's not like this is your only child.

New York: *That's low.*

Kelsey: You know if they find out I'm pregnant, I'm dead.

New York: You need to come with me. You know you don't love the girl.

Kelsey: She provides for me and I do love her. I'm just not in love with her.

New York. I can give you and the baby what you need. Come with me and we'll move to Maryland. Fuck that dyke bitch.

Kelsey: You did fuck her.

New York: I raped her bitch ass.

Kelsey: Now you are upsetting me. I told you not to do that and you did it anyway.

New York: You brought it up.

Kelsey: I did. I just had a thought. What if she's pregnant too?"

New York: She can't get pregnant. That bitch is a man. All that testosterone.

Kelsey: That was low. You know I hope the baby is a girl.

New York: You're keeping it?

Kelsey: Of course not.

New York: :-(

Kelsey: Dude you have six children by four women. This should not be a big deal to you.

New York: I'll drive you to the clinic then.

Kelsey: *Okay.*

Micky slammed the phone down hard, shattering it.

She sat on the edge of the bed, head resting in her hands. She wanted to cry, but she couldn't bring herself to cry in front of her brother and Blue. She stood and paced then ran her fingers through her locks. "So what are y'all going to do with this clown?"

"You know what we're going to do."

"Why did you bring him here?"

"I was thinking that we should kill them together."

"I thought you were going to just make her leave town?"

"Do you want me to let her go after all of this?"

Micky said, "Look, I'll handle it."

Stunna said, "Mick, now is not the time to be soft. You know if word gets out that somebody took something from me—"

"I'll handle it," Micky said then she hugged her brother.

When Micky got back to the room, Kelsey was sitting in the bed with her phone in her hand. She was surprised when Micky barged in. She sat her phone down.

"What were you doing? Texting somebody?"

"No, I was on Instagram."

"I don't believe you."

Kelsey licked her lips then rolled her eyes. "Why not?"

"Let me see your phone."

She passed her the phone. She had been on Instagram. Micky strolled through her friend list. Seeing if she had guy friends. She had a few guys, but Kelsey noticed that she had followed a host of baby sites.

"Somebody having a baby?"

"No."

"Why are you following all of these baby accounts?"

"I was just thinking that maybe one day we can adopt or we can get a sperm donor to get me pregnant. That's the only reason I followed the accounts."

"Cute baby names."

"Huh?"

"That's the name of one of the accounts you followed. Seems to me that you are thinking about naming a baby."

"I have."

"And what did you come up with?"

"Hunter."

"I like that name."

"Me too."

"What if it's a girl?"

"Madison and we can call her Maddie for short."

"Listen, why don't you cut the bullshit out? I know that you are pregnant by New York. And I know that you had gone to an abortion clinic and didn't go through with it."

"Who told you that?"

"Does it matter? Am I right?"

"You're right. I can't lie. I won't lie. I am pregnant, but I'll abort it. I was actually planning to abort it."

"Why didn't you abort it?"

"He talked me out of it."

Micky slammed her phone and it shattered into many pieces. Just like New York's phone had.

"I swear to God, I'm sorry. Mick, I'm sorry for this."

"You know what? I hate you!"

Kelsey made her way toward Micky and attempted to embrace her but Micky pushed her back.

"I love you, Micky. I'll do anything. I'll call and schedule the abortion right now."

Micky passed her a phone. "Call them. We'll get the abortion and then get out of town."

It had been a week since Tank had seen Jada after his altercation with Fresh. The swelling on his face had gone down and it was barely noticeable. When he walked in, she offered him a drink.

"I'm good."

"I didn't know you were coming."

"Yeah, it was kind of last moment."

"How you feeling?"

"I'm feeling good, but I want you to tell me where Fresh is. I can't let him get away with this."

"You want the truth?"

"Of course, I want the truth. Why wouldn't I want the truth?"

"The truth is I don't know where he lives."

"I thought you said you were going to tell the truth?" Tank's nostrils flared. He wanted to slap the fuck out of this bitch for lying.

"Honestly, I don't know where that man is. He just moved."

"Give me the old address."

"I don't know his address. I can show you where he used to live. Maybe one of his neighbors knows where he is."

"I'll drive you."

Tank was driving his wife's G Wagon. Jada sat on the passenger side with her arms crossed.

Tank asked, "What's up with the attitude? I'm the one that got fucked up."

"You know I don't want to get in that bitch's car."

"This is my car. I bought this car. Everything that she has I bought it." In the backseat, there were a bag of Flaming Hot Cheetos and two video games. She imagined that this was the family car they drove on long road trips. She wanted that life for herself.

"So, you're not talking?"

"What do you want to talk about? I'm taking you where the man used to live."

"Okay, so where do I need to go?"

"Buckhead."

"Look, Jada. I'm sorry that you had to ride in this car. You could have followed me if you wanted."

"Hey, I'm over this."

"So, if you find Fresh, what do you plan to do?"

"I'm going to hurt the motherfucker."

"Why?"

"Because he pistol-whipped me. Why do you think?"

"He hurt your pride."

"This don't have a damn thing to do with pride."

"If I hadn't been there, would you want to kill this man?"

"You were there. So I don't know how I would feel."

"I don't want nobody to get hurt. To get killed."

"You care for him?"

"I care for you."

There a brief silence then he said, "If you care for me, then you shouldn't mind showing me where this man lives. Is that the reason you are showing me where his old house is and not his new home?"

"I really don't know where this man lives. I swear he moved."

"Okay."

They rode for the next five minutes in silence except when she gave him the directions. Finally, they arrived at Fresh's address and Jada was surprised to see the BMW X6, the car that she'd turned down still in the garage.

"Somebody sure moved in fast."

"That's his car. But I don't understand. Why would he still be here?"

"Maybe he lied to you like he was moving. Or you lied to me like he was moving."

"I don't lie, Tank. Well, I don't lie for the hell of it."

"Okay."

Tank parked the car opened the glove and removed his gun.

"What the fuck are you doing?"

"What do you think I'm doing?"

"You can't do that shit right now, and you damn sure can't kill him while I'm with you or I swear to God I'm calling the police."

He placed the gun back into the glove compartment.

*****

When Willow entered Rico Suave's condo, he slapped the fuck out of her. She fell on the floor holding the side of her mouth and when she tried to stand up, he placed his Gucci loafer on her breasts, pinning her to the floor.

She nursed her jaw and said, "What did you hit me for you, asshole?"

137

"What the hell happened over there the other night?"

She shrugged to break free from his foot but couldn't.

"Look, the client was having some personal problems and he took his life."

"Why didn't you tell me where the room was? And you sounded drunk."

"He wanted to drink, so we drank. Just like I drink when I'm with you. Can you get your fucking foot off me? You're hurting my breasts."

He removed his foot and when she stood, he slapped the fuck out of her again. She covered her face and began to cry. She tried to make a move for the door and he yanked her arm.

"Where in the hell do you think you're going? I'm not finished with you yet. You still owe me, bitch."

"I'll give you your money back."

"We had a deal."

"I know and I tried my best. I really did."

"I need you to find Ava and find her fast."

"I don't think she's going to be working no more after what happened."

"Look, either you find her or you're dead."

Ava invited TeTe inside her loft and they sat in the living room and drank Zinfandel.

"What the fuck happened over there the other night?" TeTe asked.

Ava covered her face and said, "I don't want to talk about it. I'm so fucked up over this right now."

"I know you are, but I need to know what happened."

"He'd been having issues. He had a lot of shit on his mind. He was cut from the team. Football was the only thing that he knew how to do. The only thing that he was good at and when they took that away from him, the motherfucker just fell apart."

"What a shame. Did you know that he died on his birthday?"

"Yes. He kept saying that it was his birthday."

"Did the police ask any questions about the agency?"

"I don't think they knew it was an agency."

"TMZ broke the news, and they said he was partying with two friends. Your names didn't come out."

"Thank God," Ava said.

"Have you spoken or heard from Willow?"

"No."

TeTe sipped her wine. "All I know is that little half-white bitch better not be running her goddamned mouth to PoPo."

"I know. We don't want to make a bad situation worse."

TeTe removed her phone and called Willow. The phone kept going to voicemail. Then she had an idea. She called Fy-head.

"Hey, Ms. TeTe." He answered the phone in the most high-pitched, gayest voice imaginable.

TeTe said, "You remember the girl I told you to follow the other week. The one that I told you to trail to make sure she was safe?"

"Willow?"

"Yes."

"Do you know where she lives?"

"Yes. After her session, she invited me and Diamond over for drinks. She lives in a small apartment in Marietta."

"I need you to show me where she lives."

"Of course. What's wrong?"

"I tell you when you get here."

Fy-head looked a hot mess in silver spandex, high-top pink Chuck Taylors, and fuchsia-colored braids. TeTe introduced Fy-Head to Ava. They drank a glass of wine then Ava headed home. Willow lived in an apartment complex called Ivy Ridge in Building 6. It was on the third level on the unit in the back. Fy-Head knocked on the door.

"Who is it?"

"It's me, Casey."

"Casey?"

"Chile, open this door."

Willow peeked through the peephole before opening the door and then invited Fy-head, and TeTe in. They went into the living room and sat down on some ugly brown, old, rundown furniture. TeTe calculated in her mind that this ho had to have made at least twenty-five thousand dollars and she still hadn't upgraded her lifestyle.

TeTe and Fy-head were seated on the sofa and Willow sat on a leather armchair.

TeTe said, "I haven't heard anything from you since what happened the other night."

"I know. I had a lot on my mind. That was a lot to take in."

"I understand that, but we're going to have to get past that. I mean shit like that happens from time to time."

Fy-Head said, "What happened?"

"A client OD'd.

Fy-head was blowing and popping bubbles with her pink bubble gum and it was getting on TeTe's goddamned nerves. The gum popped and stuck to the side of her jaw.

Fy-head said, "Oh my God. Was your client the football player? Everybody has been talking about his OD and TMZ had one of his friends saying that he was with some call girls.

TeTe looked surprised. "One of his friends, huh?"

"Yeah."

TeTe said to Willow, "What did you tell the PoPo?"

"Oh, wait!" Willow stood and said, "Is this what this is all about? You think that I'm a rat?"

"I never said you were a rat. I just need to know what you told the police."

"I told them that it was his birthday and we were partying and having a good time and that we did a couple of lines."

"Now why the fuck did you tell them that?"

"Well, because they found the residue on his nose and found a razor blade with coke residue on it. So what was I supposed to do? Lie?"

"It's best to keep your motherfucking mouth shut in situations like this. Don't say shit."

"I didn't say that I worked for you. They never asked."

"But if they would have asked, what would you have said?"

"I don't know."

TeTe stood and walked toward the frightened girl. TeTe was about to slap the fuck out of Willow when Fy-head wedged himself between the two of them.

He was still smacking the hell out of that chewing gum and TeTe told him, "Get your fucking hands off me."

"Miss TeTe, I know you're mad. But let the girl answer the question," he said in that gay voice then the gum popped again.

TeTe sat down and regained her composure.

"You've been acting awfully strange since that day."

"I had a lot of shit on my mind."

"So what's on your mind?"

She sat down. "Look, I need your help. I need somebody to help me."

"What's wrong?"

"You remember the client that you sent me to see that had requested Ava?"

"Dildo-man?"

"Him."

"What about him?"

"He wants me to help him find Ava or else he's going to kill me."

"What?"

"Yes." She stood and ran her fingers through her hair and started pacing. "Look, I took some money from him. I know I shouldn't have taken the money, but I needed it."

TeTe said, "Slow down. What do you mean you took some money from him? You stole some money?"

"No, he paid me. He made an offer to pay me twenty-five thousand dollars. He said that he was going to give me the rest when I brought him to Ava."

"Really?"

"Yes. Please, don't kill me. I needed the money. That was the most money I had ever seen in my life. I hate that I accepted it, but I did."

"Ok, you accepted the money and agreed to take him to Ava?"

"Yeah, and the night the client OD'd, they were coming up to the hotel to kill Ava. But when they got there, the lobby was full of cops and the ambulance was there."

"Damn," TeTe said. She couldn't believe what she was hearing.
She had thought that Ava was paranoid, but it turned out that she
wasn't. She had killers after her.

"That's why I didn't answer the phone. Not that I'm hiding from
you. Not that I told the police anything. I'm hiding from Mario."

TeTe approached Willow and hugged her. The two women held on
to each other for a while until TeTe grabbed her by the throat and
began to choke the fuck out of her. Fy-head pulled her off.

Jada opened the door for Fresh and they stood and stared at
each other for twenty seconds before she invited him in. When
she closed the door, she said, "Look, I hope you didn't come to
start no bullshit, Fresh. I'm done with you."

"I came to tell you that I spoke to my attorney in Houston and I'm
turning myself in. I'm leaving tomorrow. Flying to Houston and
then I'm turning myself in. I know I can't run forever and I'm tired
of looking over my shoulder."

"I think you should. I think you will be okay in the end." Jada
thought about Tank and how he was adamant about killing Fresh.
She knew that Fresh really needed to get out of town and fast.

"You think I'll beat the case?" he asked.

"I think it will be justifiable."

"I just hope I'm able to get out on bond."

"I think you will. "

"I'm going to miss Atlanta."

"When you get the case behind you, you can come back."

"Yeah, I'm hoping. I just don't know what is going to happen. I don't want to do life in prison."

"You gotta think positive."

They exchanged smiles then he grabbed her hand and massaged it.

"Will you come see me?"

"Maybe." She didn't want to admit it, but she still liked his ass.

"I'm hoping you do."

"I don't like visiting jails. I have a half-brother in prison. I send him money, but I rarely go see him."

"You used to go see Shamari."

"That's different. That's my best friend."

He frowned, "It's true. Nobody can replace Shamari. Why don't you go and be with him?"

She turned her back. "I don't know."

"He loves you."

She knew that Shamari loved her and she loved him, but she didn't want to talk to Fresh about Shamari.

"I'd rather for you to be with Shamari than that clown-ass Tank. You're too good to be somebody's side bitch, Jada."

She laughed and said, "Coming from the man that tried to make me a side bitch too."

"My baby mother is delusional."

"Is she?"

"She's crazy."

"You made her that way."

He laughed and said, "Maybe a little."

"I just wanted to stop by and tell you that I was leaving."

"You didn't move."

"How do you know?"

"I drove by your house the other day and saw that your garage was open."

"Why didn't you come in?"

"I didn't want to do that."

He stepped toward her and hugged her. He grabbed her ass and she broke free from his grip.

"We're not going to start that again."

"Hey, I had to try. I don't know if they are going to give me a bond or not. At least, I want to remember how dat ass feel."

"Fresh, get the hell out of here."

* * * * *

Kelsey sat on the edge of the bed with her head slumped, crying when Micky entered the bedroom.

"What the hell is wrong with you?"

She looked up briefly then resumed crying.

Micky asked again. "What's wrong?"

"Nothing."

"Something is wrong."

"Micky, I'm so sorry that I did this to you. I swear you've done nothing but prove your love to me over and over and I don't deserve a person like you. I really don't."

Micky sat beside her and then said, "Well, all that is over now." She kissed Kelsey and then said, "We have to get out of here or my brother is going to come and get you."

Kelsey got up and began to pack a few things. Then she rushed into the bathroom and barfed three times. Micky entered the bathroom to see if she was okay.

"I'm fine. Just morning sickness, you know?"

"So how many weeks are you?"

"Twelve weeks."

"We have to get somewhere and get an abortion before it's too late."

"I know," Kelsey said then she vomited again. She stood up and made her way to the sink and gargled a bottle of Listerine. Then she packed a few of her belongings into a big box: jeans, shoes, blouses, and a MacBook pro. When she was finished, she sat on the bed again and opened a bag of Funyuns. She offered Micky some, but she declined. Then Micky sat down beside her as she devoured those Funyuns.

Micky said, "What are you going to do, sit here and eat Funyuns or pack?"

"I'm going to try to pack. I'm just so tired."

Micky sighed. "So you really weren't going to get the abortion. Didn't you know that I was going to find out sooner or later?"

"I had planned to get the abortion."

"Why didn't you?"

"I couldn't."

"So, you was going to carry the man's baby that raped and robbed me and my brother."

"It's not the baby's fault."

Micky said, "I can tell you were thinking about keeping this baby."

"Micky, I'll do whatever you tell me to do."

"Get rid of it."

"Just like that?"

"Are you serious? I can't believe that you are even thinking about keeping this goddamned baby!"

"I was just thinking that we can raise the baby. We can get married, me and you. Didn't you say that you wanted a baby?"

"I did."

Kelsey set the Funyuns down and used her hands to push up from the bed, leaving fingerprints on the sheets. She hugged Micky.

Micky whispered, "Let's raise the baby together."

Kelsey said, "Are you serious?"

"I am. I want to do whatever it takes to make you happy. Now let's finish packing this shit before my brother gets paranoid and come to find us."

Kelsey kissed Micky and said, "I love you so damn much."

Fresh just turned into his neighborhood home when he noticed a black G Wagon trailing him. He called Jada and she answered on the first ring.

"Hello?"

"Hey, do you know anybody that has a black G Wagon?"

"Yes, why?"

"Someone has been following me for a few miles driving a black G Wagon and I was wondering if you knew who it was."

"Oh my God. It's Tank."

"Tank?"

"Yeah."

"The nigga I pistol-whipped?"

"Yes."

"Look, I'm going to call you back." Fresh opened the glove compartment and then the armrest and realized that he'd left home without his gun.

"No. Stay on the phone with me."

"What?"

"Stay on the phone with me," Jada said. Though she really didn't want him to stay on the phone with him. She remembered the day that Lani was murdered with Jada on the phone listening. She damn sure didn't want to go through that again.

Fresh floored the BMW and the G Wagon accelerated as he turned into his neighborhood. He was going fifty-five miles per hour in a residential area. He slowed down for the curb and almost floored two runners.

A light-skinned dude with freckles and a ponytail leaned out of the G Wagon firing shots and a bullet hit the side of the car. Fresh charged past a stop sign. He stopped the car, sprang from the car, and sprinted home. His townhome was on the parallel street. He opened the fence and cut through a backyard home. A beautiful Siberian Huskie charged toward his ass but he kicked the dog in the mouth before climbing the privacy fence.

The light-skinned dude was following behind him and let off two more shots before yelling, "Bitch-assed nigga."

Tank floored the Benz wagon and sped to the street over. He parked his car on the end of Fresh's street. He anxiously awaited Fresh's dash through the neighbor's yard. Fresh emerged running for his life and Tank let off three shots. One into his quad. Fresh was two feet from his house. He approached the door and punched in the code to the combination lock 2482. The door opened and Fresh removed his cell phone and dialed 911.

"I need an ambulance. I've been shot."

Two minutes later, the police and ambulance were storming the neighborhood.

Tank and the light-skinned nigga peeled out.

Tank said, "I think I hit him but I didn't kill him."

Micky and Kelsey had just finishing packing up their things when someone knocked on the door. Micky opened the door and Stunna and Blue walked in.

Kelsey looked at Micky and said, "Micky, don't let them kill me."

Stunna moved toward Kelsey and Micky wedged herself between them and said, "I can't let you do it, bruh."

Stunna squinted then clenched his fist.

Kelsey said, "Look, I will go wherever you want me to go. Just don't hurt me."

Stunna attempted to remove Micky from in front of him.

Micky said, "I can't let you do it."

His nostrils flared.

Micky turned and faced Kelsey, yielding a knife. "Let me do it."

Kelsey backed up and dashed from the room. Micky charged after her, gripping the knife.

"Mick, you know I'm pregnant. What about the baby?"

Micky pushed that knife deep inside Kelsey's belly then ripped her throat open. Crimson colored blood sputtered, her eyes were open wide as she choked out, "I loved you."

* * * * *

A delivery man knocked on Rico Suave's Airbnb. He opened the door and the man said. "I have a delivery for Hector Gonzales."

 Rico Suave was about to say that there was no Hector Gonzales, he'd almost forgotten that was his alias. "That's me."

"I have a cake and birthday balloons."

Rico Suave signed for the red velvet cake that he'd requested from the agency. He had finally decided to take advantage of the birthday special. He'd requested Willow and the white girl that had shown up weeks earlier as well as a red velvet cake. His favorite. His grandma used to make it for him when he was small. He pointed to a table and the deliveryman sat them on the table and said, "Have an awesome birthday."

Rico Suave handed the man a twenty-dollar tip and he was gone. Seconds after the door closed, there was a knock on the door. He rushed to the door and opened it. Two curvaceous women stood in the hallway. He invited them in. After they closed the door, he asked, "Where is Willow?"

"Willow is not working this week."

"I asked for Willow."

"She's not working."

He closed the door and asked, "What's your names?"

The taller of the two said, "My name is Diamond but everyone calls me Diamond Princess."

"Diamond Princess, huh? How fucking ghetto." He walked to the other side of the room and then stared at the other woman. "What is your name?"

"I'm Cassandra."

"Well, I'm going to tell you right away I'm not interested in you two and if I didn't know any better, I would think that you were men." He laughed and then poured himself a drink.

Fy-Head said, "I thought that was what you wanted. I was told you like getting fucked in the ass."

"Get out." He brandished a .45 and pointed it at Fy-Head.

"Go ahead and kill me, I don't care about dying."

Rico Suave's eyes narrowed and said, "Look, I am not the one to play with. Leave now or else."

Diamond Princess said, "Girl, let's get out of here, I can tell he ain't playing." She grabbed Fy-Head by the arm and they made a beeline for the door.

CHAPTER 16

Stunna had rented a forty-two-foot cigarette boat. He, Blue, and Micky were at the front of the boat and New York was in the back of the boat with his hands tied with disposable restraints and his feet cased in cement. A sack was over his head, almost suffocating the man.

He had complained and Stunna had said, "It's only a matter of time before you're dead anyways."

Kelsey's corpse also had cinder block shoes. When they were out in the middle of the water, Blue tossed New York's ass over into the ocean headfirst.

Micky ran her fingers though Kelsey's hair and kissed her forehead. "I loved you, bitch," she said and tossed her over in the ocean. Stunna drove the boat full speed into the shore.

Later that night, Rico Suave was lying in the bed alone in expensive silk pajamas staring at the ceiling. This had been one of the worst birthday's he'd ever had. There was no party. No birthday dinner and he wondered if those two girls that the agency sent him were men. They were powerfully built women even more powerful than Serena Williams but they both had pretty faces. They wore way too much make up and kinda looked fake, but he regretted that he didn't at least get them to use his toy on him. The fact that Willow had obviously shared his desires with them had pissed him off. Willow had made his life more complicated. It now looked like the little trailer-park bitch had decided to betray him. He would have to kill her too. He smiled as he remembered the red velvet birthday cake. He leapt from the bed and ran to the fridge where he'd stored it after the girls had gone. He sat it on the counter and removed a knife from the drawer. He sat down at the table and sang happy birthday to himself. Then he dashed back into the kitchen to get a lighter and he lit the single blue candle and blew it as hard as he could. The last thing he heard was a thunderous boom as the cake exploded, melting away his handsome face. Rico Suave could be heard hollering two floors above as he darted into the bathroom and into the shower.

An hour later TeTe texted him from an anonymous number: *How did you enjoy the cake? Was it like grandma's?*

* * * * * * * * * * * * * *

KINGPIN WIFEY III,

Part 5: Crown My Ass

CHAPTER 1

Fresh, wearing a blue hospital gown and an IV attached to his right arm, was handcuffed to the bed. He held onto a cup of apple juice in his free hand when Jada entered the room and approached the bed. She leaned forward and kissed him. "Are you okay?" she asked.

"I'm fine. The bullet went in and out of my quadriceps."

She pecked him again on the jaw. "Thank God."

She plopped down in a small chair beside the bed. "Do you need me to call anyone, like your mom or your baby mama or anything?"

"No."

She noticed the cuffs on his wrist and frowned.

"I know," he said.

"So you're going to jail?"

"Yes, but I'm happy, Jada. I'm happy that Tank didn't kill me. I could have been dead, and I'm happy that I'm going to get this behind me so I can go on with my life."

"I think you're going to be okay."

He shot her a fake smile and said, "I think so, too."

There was an awkward silence. They both cared an awful lot about each other but they knew they couldn't coexist. They were players. Jada wasn't used to being played.

Fresh sipped the apple juice then he buzzed the nurse. A stout black woman named Clarice burst through the door, shaking her head. "And what do you want with me now, Mr. Fresh?"

Jada laughed and said, "You know his nickname?"

Clarice said, "He told me to call all him Fresh and started telling the whole staff about why the Texans were better than the Falcons and then started telling me how I reminded him of his auntie, talking about I was "Trill" whatever that means, trying to charm me so I can get him extra apple juice."

Fresh smiled. "It worked." Then he said, "Ms. Clarice, can you please get maintenance to come up here and fix my TV? The Texans game about to come on."

Clarice placed her hands on her hips. "We don't watch no Texans 'round here. You're in Atlanta, Mr. Fresh."

Fresh said, "Pretty please with sugar on top."

Clarice looked at Jada and said, "How you put up with this man?"

"I don't."

"Smart woman." Clarice passed him two more juices and said she would call the utility man. Then she disappeared.

Fresh looked at Jada and said, "What's up with Shamari?"

"Haven't spoken to him in a while."

"I want to introduce him to the plug."

"What about Q?"

"I don't think Q wants to do this anymore, plus he's facing murder charges."

"Why would you do this for Shamari?"

"You don't think he can handle it?"

"I know he can, but the question is does he want to handle it. I know he just got out too and I don't think he's trying to get caught up in the streets like Black was."

"I'm not worrying about that."

"Well, I am. I don't want Shamari to get killed."

"You love that man, don't you?"

"I do."

"Jada, I love you, but I don't think you're going to be happy until you get back with him."

"He has someone now."

"But you two belong together." He paused. "You know I'm right."

"I don't want to talk about that right now."

"Can you call Gordo for me?"

"Now?"

"Yes."

"Why?"

"I want to tell him what to do."

"What is his number?"

"281-456-5789."

Jada dialed the number.

"Buena?" Gordo answered the phone on the second ring.

"Gordo? This is Jada, can you hold on for a second? Fresh wants to speak to you." She turned to Fresh then pressed the phone against his face.

"I got in a little trouble."

"Trouble?"

"Yes, listen closely." Fresh went on to explain that he wanted him to meet Shamari and for him to get in touch with Jada when he came to Atlanta. She would give Gordo the money that he was owed.

Gordo thanked him and assured him that he would be there for him if he needed him.

Jada placed her phone in her purse.

Fresh lusted after her. She was wearing a black body suit with five-inch heels. He wanted to call Clarice and offer her a thousand dollars to guard the door while he fucked Jada for ten minutes. But he knew that Jada would oppose it, and it was just a matter of time before the police came back to haul his ass off to jail.

Jada walked in the direction of the door and he called her. She turned and faced him.

"Thank you for all you have done for me while I've been here in Atlanta," he said.

"Don't sweat it."

"One more thing."

"What is it?"

"I love you, Jada."

She stared at him for a few seconds. She couldn't't believe what he'd just said. Moments earlier he was telling her that she would be happy with Shamari. She didn't't respond because she knew it was a lie. Fresh was a player and he would always be a player, incapable of loving any one, but he had been right about one thing. She loved Shamari but he was in love with another woman.

*****

Shantelle was naked. She had just stepped out of the shower and was applying coconut oil to her skin when the doorbell rang. She looked at her phone. It was 10:13 p.m. She said, "Who is it?" She entered the living room and was about to look through the peephole.

"It's me, Q. Open up. I need to talk to you."

"Just give me a minute," she said then she disappeared into the room and returned wearing a bathrobe. She opened the door. He stepped inside and she said, "What brings you here so late?"

"I'm sorry for barging in your spot like this, but I need your help and I need it right away."

She led him into the living room and offered him a seat. He declined. Instead, he paced and she sat down on the sofa. "What's up, Q?"

"Look, I know who has been textingJessica Turner."

"Who's Jessica Turner?"

"Trey's baby mama."

"Oh, I never knew her last name. Who text her?"

"Monte."

"What? This doesn't't make any sense and how did he get a phone inside the prison."

"I don't know where You've been or who you know, but everybody has a cell phone in prison. Look, my attorney's P.I. found out that the phone was located near the prison. I know it's Monte because I gave the phone to Trey and I forgot about it. I'm sure he must have given it to Monte."

"Damn. OK, but how can I help?"

"I need you to go to the police and tell them that Trey gave Monte the phone and you know that Monte influenced Jessica and not me."

"Why do you want me to do that and not you?"

"I'm cartel affiliated and if I go to the police, I'm dead. If I talk to them about anything and they find out, I'm dead."

She looked concerned. "I see."

"Look, I need you to do this. I need you to clear my name, please."

She stood and he could see her silhouette through the robe. She worked out way too much for him and that damn tiny waist looked great, and he was aroused.

She caught him looking but pretended not to notice. She turned and faced him. "What the fuck is in this for me, Q?"

"What do you want?"

"I want what Starr has."

"And what is that?"

"I want my own business. If I go do this for you, Q, I want you to help me get a fitness studio and I need money for equipment."

"How much do you need?"

"At least fifty thousand dollars."

He made eye contact with her. "Do this for me and I'll give you seventy-five thousand dollars. And I'll pay the rent for your studio for one year. I gotta get these charges dropped on me. I gotta get the fuck out of the game."

"Do you think you can stay out of the game?"

"I should have been out years ago. I have enough money to last me for a while. So do we have a deal?"

She nodded then disappeared into the kitchen. His eyes followed her body. He had to admit Shantelle had a sexy-ass walk. She dropped the robe and his eyes were now focused on her clean-shaved kitty. He propped her up on the counter, dropped his pants then entered her doggy-style.

She yelled, "Smack my ass!"

He yanked her hair and slapped her ass and forced his tool as far he could inside her. The sound of his thighs whacking her ass cheeks aroused him even more.

She said, "You...make...me...feel...so...good."

He flipped her onto her back and she shoved her tongue in his mouth. She gave him very wet kisses. Her newly painted nails clawed his back, and her mouth traveled from his lips to his neck. She bit into his neck slightly and he stopped and frowned.

She laughed a little before saying, "Don't want Starr to find out, huh?"

"Whatever."

She licked his nipple before biting it. He was turned on further. He entered her again missionary and she could feel him swell inside her.

"This...dick...is...so...good...Q."

He kept stroking and she whispered in his ear, "I want to be nasty."

"Huh?"

"I want to do something nasty to you."

She kneeled and took him in her mouth. Then she removed it and looked then spat on it and took him inside her mouth again toying with his balls then swallowed them before spitting them out. Her tongue was now in the crease of his ass. He tightened his ass cheeks and she laughed.

His hands held onto her head and she licked his inner thighs. Her tongue traveled his thigh, then his shin, then his calf. She lifted his foot and lodged his toe in her mouth. He wiggled his foot free and said, "You don't have to do this."

"I want to. Let me do what I want to do it. I want to submit to you, Q. I've always dreamed of being submissive to you."

He smiled and held his toe to her mouth.

After she was done devouring his big toe. She stood up and removed a set of handcuffs from the kitchen drawer. She cuffed herself to the back of the kitchen chair and said, "Rape me."

*****

B.C. was returning to his UPS truck when Stunna appeared in his view. Startled, he stepped back and thought about running away. He hadn't seen Stunna since the Feds had taken his package. And that had worried him. Stunna had tried to call him a few times, but he didn't answer the phone. He didn't want to talk to him, and he damn sure didn't want to see him. He had thought about leaving Atlanta. He had a few thousand dollars saved but how long would it last? In the end, he'd decided to stay but now coming face to face with Stunna, he didn't know if he'd made the best decision.

 Stunna grinned at him and said, "You haven't been answering my calls. You been avoiding your big brother?"

"No, not at all. As a matter of fact, I was going to call you today."

A black Benz Sprinter was situated across the parking lot with eight niggas in it. Micky sat behind the wheel. Stunna said, "You see that van full of dudes over there?"

"Yeah."

"I need you to go get in the back of the van."

"I can't just abandon my truck. I have a truck full of boxes that need to be delivered."

"You can and you will." Stunna wanted to slap the shit out of him but decided not to. "Call your supervisor and tell them that your wife had an emergency and you have to go home."

B.C. removed his cell phone from his pocket then dialed his supervisor and informed him that his wife and kids had been in a car accident and he was heading to the hospital. His supervisor asked him for the location of the truck and said that he was going to send someone to pick up the truck. B.C. walked over and leapt into the Benz Sprinter and they drove to one of Stunna stash houses in Cobb County. B.C recognized the men. Most of the men he had seen the last time he   and they drug his ass inside the house.

B.C. pleaded with Micky. "Please don't let him kill me. I didn't tell the Feds shit. I swear to God."

"I didn't say you did. As a matter of fact, I know you didn't."

Stunna placed a Glock .40 to B.C.'s forehead. Next, he stripped B.C. down to his tightie whitey underwear and then forced B.C. to remove them as well. Stunna lashed B.C.'s ass eighteen times with an extension cord. B.C. hollered like a stray animal.

The whip hitting his legs hurt like hell as he held onto his legs to soothe the pain. It did nothing, but somehow it made him feel better.

"So you know that I didn't tell them shit and you still want to whip my ass. I don't get it."

"First, that wasn't the Feds that took my shit; it was some clown-ass niggas. But if it were the Feds, you should have told me the first time. You lied to me telling me some bullshit story about you lost my package.

"I know and I'm sorry, but I didn't know what else to do."

Stunna stared at the defenseless nude man lying on his back squirming. "Get yo punk ass up and put your clothes on."

B.C. stood, his shriveled dick swinging. He glanced at Stunna, afraid that Stunna was going to slap the shit out of him again. He crept to the other side of the room to find his UPS uniform, along with his socks piled in the corner. After he was fully clothed, he stood in the center of the circle of men.

Stunna approached B.C. and handed him the keys to the Porsche that Stunna had taken from B.C. a month ago.

Stunna said, "Your car is outside."

"You're giving me my car back?" B.C narrowed his eyes. A few minutes earlier, he was getting his ass whipped with an extension cord and now he was being handed the keys to his car back.

"What does it look like?"

"Thank you."

"Are you ready to go back to work?"

"Well, I'm going back tomorrow."

"Not what I mean. I have a big shipment coming. I need you to catch it on your route for me."

"Whatever you say."

"It's not whatever I say. If this shit doesn't make it, you're dead. This is on consignment from the plug."

"Look, I'll do my best. You know I'm loyal to you."

 Stunna slapped the fuck out of him. "If you were loyal, you would haven't lied to me."

B.C. held unto his jaw and said, "What if someone steals the package before it gets to me?"

"You have no control over that. If that doesn't happens, you get to live." Stunna grinned.

A fat Mexican with a handlebar mustache was sitting on Jada's couch eating fried chicken and Mac and Cheese and drinking a Welch's grape soda when Shamari entered. The man stood and extended his hand.

Jada said, "Shamari, this is my friend Gordo."

Shamari's left eyebrow rose.

Gordo swabbed chicken grease from the corner of his mouth. "Jada and Fresh tell me you're a good person."

Shamari glanced at Jada and asked, "What the hell is going on?"

"Fresh is in jail."

"Ok, that explains why he hasn't been answering the phone."

"He got shot and went to the hospital and they had the warrant there waiting on him."

"Who shot him?"

"It's a long story." There was no way that Jada was going to tell Shamari that it was over a fight with Tank that happened at her home.

"He going to be okay?"

Gordo said, "Don't worry, Shamari, I come to help."

Shamari stared at the tub of lard-assed Mexican who looked a hot mess in a plaid shirt, cowboy boots, and a huge cowboy belt buckle.

Gordo finished his food and Jada offered him more. He declined and thanked Jada.

Shamari plunged into the armchair parallel to Gordo and said, "Jada, what is going on?"

"Fresh is going to be gone for a while and Gordo needs another partner."

 Shamari locked eyes with Gordo. "So you want me to work for you?"

"I say we work together. I'll give you the best price you ever had. Jada and Fresh tell me that you are a standup guy."

Jada delivered Shamari a can of Pepsi and after he opened it, he said to Gordo, "Thanks for the opportunity, but I just got out of prison."

"I know."

Shamari narrowed his eyes. "So how much are we talking?"

"A thousand kilos. Maybe two. I want to make you a rich man."

"That's too much."

"I don't understand. Why would you turn down an opportunity?"

"I don't want to be linked with the cartel. Not right now." A few years ago he would have jumped at this opportunity, but he didn't want to go back to prison. He didn't want to let his sister down. It would destroy her if he got into more trouble. He planned to go totally legit in a few months and he knew that you just didn't quit working for the cartel.

"Cartel is what the government calls us, but I like to think of us as friends."

"I'm trying to get out of this business."

Gordo laughed. "Nobody gets out of the business. We all say that or think that but the truth is, Shamari, we don't have a choice."

"I have my family to worry about. My sister was by my side the whole time I was locked up and I don't want to disappoint her."

"You're still in the game. I don't understand."

"I am a freelancer, meaning I want to be able to deal with whoever I want to deal with. I don't need or want the cartel controlling me."

Gordo extended his hand and said, "I appreciate you coming to meet with me." Then he looked at Jada and asked if there were any more wings and potato salad left.

Jada smiled and said, "Sure there is." Then she bee lined to the kitchen thinking that Gordo knew damn well his fat ass had wanted more from the start. She didn't know why he'd declined her offer for seconds five minutes earlier.

*****

She was the cutest little girl with pink ribbons decorating her braids and dressed in a pink Hello Kitty shirt and jeans standing at the door. JUJU ON THAT BEAT was blasting from her headphones. She pointed to Shamari and said, "You ugly. You yo Daddy's son." Then she danced in a circle.

Shamari said, "What?"

She removed her Beats headphones and said, "It's a song."

Shamari asked her what her name was.

"My name is Butterfly," she said. "What's yours?"

"Shamari."

"Are you going to be my mama's new boyfriend?"

"No." He laughed then asked, "Why do you ask?"

"Because she needs a new boyfriend. Her last boyfriend was really, really black, and we called him Black and he died. Well, he got killed and Mommy was really sad for a while until one day I bought her an Italian Ice and gave her a paper chain that I had made and she's been happy ever since. But I want her to get a boyfriend, not a really, really black one, but a light-skinned one like you. But Black was cool and he always gave me money. Do you have any money to give me?"

 "No."

"Well, you probably won't work with Mommy cuz she like money and I like money too and I'm going to grow up to marry a baseball player like Evelyn cuz they got the most money."

"Evelyn? Who is Evelyn?"

"She played on Basketball Wives. First, she had a basketball player then she got a football player then she found out that baseball players had more money. Then she married one of them. But all she had to do was Google then she would known right off that baseball players had all the money."

 Shamari was laughing his ass off. "How old are you little girl?"

"Almost nine."

"Nine going on forty," TeTe said from the top of the stairs.

Shamari made eye contact with TeTe who looked amazing standing atop the spiral staircase. She was wearing a crème Hermes pantsuit with heels. He watched her as she walked down the stairs and when they were face to face she said, "I see you met Ms. Butterfly."

"Yes."

Butterfly said, "Mommy, he's broke."

TeTe pointed to the stairs. "Go to your room."

Butterfly frowned and said, "But you said that I could ride my bicycle."

"Okay, well then go outside and ride your bicycle and you better not go out in the street."

Butterfly pushed her bicycle outside. TeTe said, "I'm surprised to see you."

"Can we sit down?"

"This must be serious."

"I just need to get to the bottom of something."

He followed her into the living room and when they were seated, he asked, "What's up with Ava?"

"What do you mean?"

"She's my lady."

"I know this already."

"Can I trust her?"

"I guess you can."

Shamari sighed and said, "I don't know how else to ask this, but has she been fucking around on me? I know she's been working for you."

"She was honest with you about that."

Shamari stood and paced and said, "I don't know. There's just something I can't figure out about this girl. I mean she shows up in town and she tells me that she has stolen money from D-Boys and they are out to kill her and that she's been fucking and sleeping with old white men for money."

"Whoa. Shamari. You have no right to judge that woman. How many bitches have you slept with? All that matters is that she is your woman now and I can tell you this, she is loyal."

 "How do you know that?"

"Because I've offered her money to meet with clients and she refused because of your relationship."

"Okay, but what about this shit with that football player?"

TeTe stood and strolled over to the bar where she poured herself a glass of Riesling.

"I'm so stressed right now."

"Why?"

"TMZ was outside my home trying to get me to talk about it. Someone tipped them off that I'm the madam that sent the girls to meet him."

"Well, you are, aren't you?"

"Don't you see this shit is going to hurt my business so bad? Nobody is going to want to fuck with me. My clients want discretion. They don't want to be all over the news. My reputation is definitely going to take a hit."

 Shamari said, "I get that, but back to what I was saying about Ava."

"Ava hasn't fucked anyone. Nobody. She's only had two clients. The football player and this other guy. An old black guy that wants to masturbate. He's been my client for years and all he likes to do is choke his chicken around pretty girls."

"So this is supposed to be a good thing?"

"The question is, have you been good?"

"What is that supposed to mean?"

"You know one of my friends sent me a Me-Me with a saying that 'Men like a good girl to come home to after a long day of cheating'."

"What the hell is a Me-Me? Do you mean a meme?"

"You know what the hell I'm talking about. Anyway, men want a perfect woman, so they can do all the cheating they want to do. I know you're not faithful." She glanced between his legs and stole a look at this package. It was limp but she could tell it had some size to it.

"You're a friend of Black's so I know you're a ho."

"Is that so?"

"Hell, yeah." She sipped her wine and said, "Damn, I miss that black motherfucka. He was the first man to fuck me good in a very long time."

Shamari laughed.

"Seriously, Shamari, I don't know what I'm going to do. I only have a little bit of money saved up."

"When you say a little, what do you have?"

"I have a couple of hundred thousand dollars but I know that is not going to last long. I have to do something."

He stood and said, "You ever sold coke?"

 "Eighties, early nineties. I ain't getting involved in that shit. The risk is not worth the reward."

"But what if it is?" His eyes lit up.

 "What do you mean?"

 "I met an esse and he wanted to give me a thousand kilos."

"Why didn't you take them then?"

"I don't want to be that deep."

 "I see."

"What does he want for them?"

 "I don't know. I can find out if you're interested. As a matter of fact, I'll call him and introduce you to him."

"I really don't want to do it."

She sipped her wine. The doorbell rang. Seconds later, Butterfly came running into the room and said, "Mommy, it's the news people again, and they are out there with all the cameras and stuff."

TeTe said, "Make the introduction."

*****

Fat-ass Gordo was chomping down on a ribeye prepared medium well and the motherfucker had the nerve to have a loaded baked potato with sour cream and butter spilling from it. The napkin tucked into his shirt covered his rotund belly and TeTe stared at his fat little pudgy fingers thinking to herself how disgusting this man must look naked.

She hated to see men with fat little fingers. Probably had a mound of hair covering his belly and she could imagine what his farts must be like. Yuck! She introduced herself then sat in the booth beside Shamari.

"You can call me Gordo." He smiled and she thought that at least he had a nice set of teeth. His perfect teeth sparkled but she knew that good dental work in Mexico was very cheap.

"I'm TeTe."

"Where is your boyfriend?"

"Boyfriend? My boyfriend died."

 Gordo cut his eyes at Shamari. "I thought that you had someone for me to meet that I could trust."

 TeTe laughed. "That would be me, sir."

"But you're a woman. A very good looking woman." He laughed.

"What does that have to do with anything?"

"I don't deal with women."

 "And why not?"

"Women are weak. Women are soft."

"Oh darling, you ain't ever met a woman like me."

"Oh yeah?"

"Really."

"This is the big time. This is not small-time hustling."

"I understand."

Gordo diced the steak into tiny pieces and then he said, "In this business, you have to kill. Do you have a problem with that?"

She smiled and said, "Like I said, you ain't ever seen a woman like me."

Gordo continued to slice up his steak. When he was done, he smiled. "I like you."

"Good, so are we going to work together?"

He took a swig of water. "I don't know. It depends."

"Depends on what?"

He looked up from his plate and said, "I need someone murdered. I don't care if you do it or not, but I want you to make sure it happens."

There were potatoes buried inside Gordo's mustache and she picked up her napkin and wiped the side of her face to indicate to him the location that he needed to wipe. "You have food in your 'stache."

"Gracias." He cleaned his mustache.

"So who do you want me to slay?"

He laughed. "So it's that simple for you?"

"Very simple. Like I said, you ain't ever met a woman like me before."

"Well, this guy owes my friend a debt. Not a personal debt of mine. I don't know anyone in Atlanta except Fresh and Q. Do you know them?"

"I don't. I've heard of them. You want me to take them out?"

He laughed and said, "No, these are my friends."

 Shamari laughed. Though he'd heard about TeTe, this was the first time he'd witnessed for himself how crazy she was.

"My friend Carlos consigned this guy thirty kilos. He gave him a month to pay, but it has been six months and he hasn't received his money yet."

"I don't kill kids. If you want me to hurt a child, I simply can't do that, but I'll light every other motherfucka in that house up." TeTe smiled.

Gordo laughed. "Do the job and I'll give you ten kilos so we can start our relationship."

"The job is done."

CHAPTER 3

His name was Dante Small, but he was anything but small. Dante was six foot three and almost three hundred pounds. He'd gone to Auburn on a football scholarship in college and his body used to be composed of solid muscle but for the last eight years all he did was trap and party. Inside the VIP Section of V-live he sat at a table with four strippers and two of his friends. He'd already blown forty thousand dollars on Ace of Spade champagne and making it rain. The strippers: Honey, Sunshine, Crystal, and Rainsat on each of his boys' laps.

When Yo Gotti's song came on, a woman approached him, wearing a pink backless dress. She walked up to him and extended her hand and said, "What's your name?"

His eyes settled on her waist and her ass trying to determine if her ass was fake. This was Atlanta and nobody was real, but what the fuck did he care? The woman was fine. He introduced himself as Dante and she said her name was Princess.

 He guided her past the velvet rope and his eyes landed on her breasts. He wanted to rip that pink backless body dress off her right there in VIP.

 He poured her a glass of champagne. Two of the strippers rolled their eyes at the new bitch getting the attention from the man with the most money. Oftentimes the dancers at the club resented the civilian girls who were patrons. The attitude was that they were taking money out of their pockets.

She sipped her champagne and crossed her legs and he found himself staring at her high heels. She was so goddamned feminine and he liked that.

She said, "You've been blowing a lot of money in here."

"When you got it like me, you don't give a fuck about money, baby. My motto is money is to be spent."

Her smile was infectious and he found himself smiling hard as hell. His eyes flashed.

"So what does a girl have to do to get your attention?"

"You have it."

"Is that so?" She sipped her champagne and then batted her long lashes. She unzipped her dress slightly and he could imagine the perfect boobies underneath. When she saw him staring, she took her hand and rubbed her breast.

A Drake song was playing and all of his boys were getting lap dances and a flurry of bills rained down in the section.

He said, "Why are you here and where are you from?"

"Where do I look like I'm from?"

"I don't know, like maybe New York or Cali or Texas. I don't know, but I know you ain't from Atlanta."

"I'm from Stone Mountain, baby. I've been on the West Coast for the past two years, but I'm a Georgia Peach."

She massaged his thigh then fondled his tool. "Let's go to the bathroom."

His mouth flew open. "I can't go into the women's bathroom."

"I'll go into the men's bathroom."

"What's going to happen in the bathroom?"

"Lead the way and you'll find out."

He took hold of her hand and they walked to the bathroom. Nine men lined up in front of the bathroom. He peeled off nine one hundred dollar bills and gave each man a hundred dollars to let him cut the line. He led her into the bathroom. The scent of the bathroom was disgusting.

The attendant was a sixty-five year old grey haired man with a thick mustache. He stood in front of a table filled with breath mints, gum, cologne, toothpaste, deodorant, and a number of other hygienic products. He tipped the attendant, held onto her hand and they entered the stall. When the door closed, they heard a tap on the door.

The attendant tossed a clean white towel over the stall and said, "I don't know, but I thought you might need this, partner."

"Thanks."

She placed the towel on the floor of the stall and kneeled, and unbuckled his belt. She removed his tool. He dropped his pants then lowered his underwear below his knees. She took his shaft inside her hand then licked it before taking him deep in her mouth. He put his hands on her head. He'd just met this bitch and she was sucking him off here in a bathroom stall. What a slut, but he was aroused. Somebody tapped on the stall.

"What the hell is going on in there?" the guy said then laughed.

The attendant said, "Mind your own damn business."

Dante forced his dick down her throat.

Two condoms rained down into the stall and the attendant said, "Just in case you need them."

He stooped to pick up the Gold Magnum packet and ripped it open with his mouth—a condom that seconds earlier had been on a floor that reeked of urine and bleach. His package damn sure wasn't big enough for a Magnum, but he wasn't about to put on the smaller condom. His pride simply wouldn't allow that. She toyed with his balls as he bullied the over-sized condom onto his penis head. He then exposed her massive breasts with perfect nipples. He placed his mouth over her tits and attempted to undo her dress, but she resisted.

"Let's go back to your place." She kissed him and all he could think about was how she'd just sucked his dick and he wondered how many times she'd met strangers. How many times had she fucked men in bathroom stalls?

He uttered, "Baby, I want to fuck you right now."

"But the bathroom is crowded now."

The attendant said, "You can fuck as long as you want and I'll make sure nobody bothers you." Then he said, "You're gonna take care of me, right?"

"I got ya, pops," he said.

"Fuck as long as you want."

Princess said, "I want to be able to please you, and I'd rather be in a bed."

His dick throbbed. He removed the condom and she stroked him with her hands.

The old attendant said, "Girl, you need to quit playing and go on and break that man off."

Dante tossed the condom in the bathroom toilet and then flushed it.

She said, "How about I suck you until you come and then we go back to your place?"

She returned to her position and he placed his dick between her mountainous tits and fucked them until he came all over her chin. She slurped every damn drop of his semen up.

Later that night, they were in his townhome in midtown lying in the bed and he was puffing a blunt when she asked, "How am I going to get back home?"

He inhaled the blunt and said, "Home? What do you mean home? Shawty, you just got over here."

She smiled and said, "After we're done."

"I'll take you home or you can get an Uber."

"I'll take an Uber. I need to go back to get my car that's at the parking lot of the club."

"Whatever. We'll worry about that later." He passed her the blunt. She took a hit really fast then passed it back to him.

He frowned and said, "Did you even inhale?"

"I'm really not a smoker. I like to drink."

He smiled. "What would you like to drink?"

"Do you have vodka?"

"I got Absolut."

"That will do."

He darted into the kitchen to get the vodka. Seconds later, he returned and he passed her the glass of vodka.

"So how many times have you sucked a man off in a bathroom?"

"Oh, only one other time. And there has to be magnetism for me to act like that."

"You're attracted to me?"

"I am. You're a very attractive man."

He took a toke from the blunt and as the smoke entered his lungs, he hacked and barked—he was smoking Moonrock; some really strong shit that he'd gotten from L.A. He sat the blunt down on the Budweiser can on the nightstand. She stood and strolled to the other side of the room to pick up the remote lying on a chair by the window. She powered on the TV and asked, "Can we watch Netflix? The new season of NARCOS is out and I wanna check it out."

"Look, shawty, I didn't bring you hear to watch NARCOS."

"I know."

"Well, if you know, why did you ask me that?"

"There is something I want to tell you."

"What?"

"I have a man."

"Look, I ain't trying to be your man. You can keep your man." He laughed. "These hoes ain't loyal."

"I'm very loyal."

"Why are you here?"

"Look, he had a baby outside of the relationship and I found out about it."

"So you meet me at the strip club and suck me off in the bathroom and now you are here."

"Yes, and I know what I'm here for."

"Do you?"

She smiled and then proceeded to the other side of the bed. She removed the blunt from the beer can and took a quick puff. Then sat on the bed and kissed him.

"Do you have any wine? I don't think this vodka is going to relax me," she asked.

"As a matter of fact, I got some cheap wine. You know the kind that you get from the convenience store? That Barefoot brand. Cheap bullshit?"

"It's in the fridge?"

"Yeah."

He watched her sexy ass stroll into the kitchen. She returned with the wine and sat on the bed. He put his hand on her thigh and removed her bra.

She said, "I'm a transexual."

"A what?"

"I was born a man."

Dante reached for his gun. There was no way that he was going to let this bitch live. She had sucked his dick in a bathroom stall and though nobody knew that this had happened, he knew it had happened and there was no way to resolve the issue except to take the bitch's life.

When she saw him reaching for the gun, she dashed out of the room and locked the door. He pursued and charged the bedroom door, smashing it into pieces. TeTe waited on his ass as he exited the bedroom; she pumped three shots in his chest with a 9.mm with a built in silencer. She would sell the ten kilos for twenty thousand dollars apiece. This would be the quickest two hundred thousand dollars she'd made in her life. She called Gordo when they left Dante's house.

*****

Starr snapped a couple of mirror selfies to post on social media. She looked cute and wanted to show off a little. Dressed in leggings and YSL heels, she put her hair in a simple bun that exposed her face and applied some blush and this new lipstick called Sex Machine.

 Later that evening when Stunna came to visit, he said, "Baby, you're looking like a motherfucking star. Like Gabrielle Union. I take that back. Gabby ain't got shit on you."

She smiled. She loved it when he paid her compliments.

She asked, "Did you take care of your business in South Carolina?"

"I did."

"So Micky is back?"

"She is."

"Good. Look, I have to tell you something, and I know you're not going to be happy about it, but I don't believe in playing games."

"What is it?"

"Look, I'm in love with you and Q."

He scowled. "What do you mean that you're in love with me and Q?"

"He came over and I just saw how much T.J. loved him and missed him and I just found out that he didn't murder Trey, so I just think I was being unfair to him." She paused then said, "Look, I'm sorry if you feel led on. I would feel the same way if I were you."

Stunna paced. He wanted to grab her and shake her. How could she make him fall in love with her and now tell him that she is in love with Q too? He was trying to make sense of it all. While he appreciated her for being honest, but he was crushed right now.

"Just like that? You're back with him?"

"I'm not with anyone. I was just telling you how I feel. First of all, you and I aren't together."

"That's all bullshit. You just said that you could understand why I felt like I was led on. We've slept together and You've shared with me things that I hoped that you haven't shared with everyone else. I've told you about things that I haven't told anyone."

Starr saw the pain in the man's face and she felt horrible for having to tell him what she'd just told him. She couldn't go on without facing the facts.

Stunna threw his hands up. "This is really fucked up."

"I'm not saying I don't want to be with you."

"What are you saying? You can't have both of us, baby."

"I know." She dropped her head.

"Why don't you just kick it with him? I see you have feelings for him and he is good with your son. Your son misses him and if he's going to be T.J.'s life, I think that would be good for him."

Starr sighed. "I have feelings for you too."

Stunna said, "This is crazy. So you want to be with both of us? That's not possible." Stunna embraced her then whispered, "You need to try to work it out with him." Then walked toward the door with his head down.

She watched him walk away and then she called out, "Don't leave me."

He opened the door and left shaking his head.

*****

It was 1:10 p.m. when Jada and Shamari met at Houston's for lunch. She wore distressed jeans that she'd gotten from a boutique in Phipps Plaza called Pressed. She really didn't like the outfit, but Rasheeda, the owner of the shop, was nice and had agreed to take a picture with her so she felt like supporting her. She liked that she could help another black woman out. Shamari seemed to love the little basic outfit.

He said, "You look so damn good right now."

She slid into the booth and the waitress showed up shortly afterward and poured them both water. She ordered a salmon salad and he ordered a burger with fries.

"So what's up, Jada?"

"First, how did the meeting go with Gordo and TeTe?"

"He likes her and they are going to work good together."

"Good, I think she'll be perfect for it."

"Yeah, he was a little hesitant at first."

"Why, because she's a woman?"

"Exactly."

"But she's no ordinary woman."

He laughed and said, "That's exactly what she said."

"It's true."

The waitress dropped the food off and disappeared. Shamari bit into his burger.

Silence.

"So do you miss Fresh?"

 "A little bit. Why?"

"I think he'll be fine. If it happened the way that he said it did, I think he will be okay."

"Yeah."

She reached across the table and plucked two fries from his plate and dipped them into a pool of ketchup.

"So what brings you here?" he asked. "I know you didn't come here to talk about TeTe."

"No."

He stuffed three fries into his mouth and said, "What's up?"

"You're gaining weight." Her eyes settled onto his midsection.

"Cut the bullshit, Jada. What do you need?"

She made eye contact with him. "I love you, Shamari, and I'm in love with you, Shamari."

He laughed and said, "You love me because your little boyfriend is gone or you love me because I have somebody else?"

"Look, Fresh even realized that I loved you and he said that I should be with you."

He kept chewing his food, not quite knowing what to make of what she had said. "What happened with you and Fresh?"

"Fresh was fun. Fresh was cool, but I'm at an age where I want more than being fun and cool. You're my best friend, Mari." She looked away. "I know I'm putting myself out there, but honestly this is how I feel. I don't believe there is another man out there who is going to understand me."

"Jada, you know how I feel about you."

"But?"

"I have somebody and you made it clear to me that you didn't want me when I first got out of prison."

With her fork, she toyed with her salad. She didn't want to eat. She was hungry, but she couldn't eat.

"I know what I said and I'm sorry about that. I really am."

He looked confused. "Where is all of this coming from?"

"I thought about it once you started getting serious with that Ava chick."

He laughed and said, "Oh, now I see. You don't want me to be with Ava. You don't want Ava to have me." He laughed.

"Stop laughing, Shamari. You're hurting my feelings."

"I'm sorry about that, but I'm just calling it like I see it."

"I don't think she deserves someone like you, but this is not what it is about."

"What is about then?"

"I don't want to grow old without you. You're my best friend."

He chomped down his burger. The waitress appeared and re-filled their water glasses and then left.

Shamari said, "I have a question to ask you?"

"Ask me anything."

"So it's over between you and Fresh?"

"It's over as far as I'm concerned."

"So you're not seeing anybody else. I know you, Jada, and you're a very sexual person. When was the last time you had sex?"

"Come on, Shamari. Grow the fuck up. Do you really want me to answer that question?"

"Of course I do."

"Well if you must know, it was about two weeks ago."

"Who was it with?"

"Tank."

"Who the fuck is Tank?"

"A nobody. Somebody I don't love."

"But you fucked him?"

"Hey, a girl has needs too."

"Why ain't you with him?"

"The man is married and Tank is another one that I can have fun with but I really can't see myself with."

"One more question."

"Yeah."

"Did you ever fuck Black?"

There was a long silence and she looked away and she finally resumed eye contact then said, "Yes. The last day of his life. I fucked him. It happened. I want to keep it real with you. But the whole time you were accusing me of fucking him, I wasn't. I got weak one night. We fucked and that was that. Let that man rest in peace."

He appeared stone faced with his lips pressed together.

"I know this hurt you but you asked and I couldn't lie to you. No more lies."

He set his burger on his plate. "You damn right it does, but Black is gone and I hope he's resting in peace. Doesn't change how I felt about him."

"Good because it just happened. I love you, Shamari, and if you give me another chance, I swear on everything, I'll be faithful to you. I'll be the woman that you would want me to be. I mean it's not like You've been perfect. You've cheated on me a few times too."

"But I've never slept with a friend of yours."

"I know." Her shoulders were hunched and her eyes were misty. She tried her best not to cry, but she'd just hurt her best friend. She didn't like that, but he had asked the question and since she was putting everything on the line, she had to be truthful.

He ate his fries in silence and she barely touched her salad.

Finally, he said, "I want to try to make it work with Ava."

She stood up and fought through her tears. "Okay, I understand." She rushed out of the restaurant and walked to the valet. She was still crying when the valet brought her the car. She tipped the young man five dollars.

He said, "I hope the rest of your day is better, ma'am."

She thanked the valet and screeched out of the parking lot.

When Q walked into Shantelle's home, he asked her, "Did you do what I asked you to do?"

"Yes. I went to the police and I sat with them for four hours and they were interrogating the hell out of me, asking me all kind of questions about Monte and Trey's relationship and asked me if I sold drugs. Asked me why was I with Monte on the day he got busted. A Fed came in and told me that you were a big-time drug trafficker that they have been watching for years. Asked me why was I trying to clear your name."

"And what did you say?"

"I said it wasn't about clearing your name, but about clearing my conscience."

"And did they go for it?"

"I don't know, but I told them that it was Monte that encouraged Jessica to kill Trey."

Q started pacing and then he stopped and looked at her. "Thank you so much."

"You're going to hold up your end of the bargain, right? I mean I found a space that I want to rent for my studio."

"Yes, of course."

"Did you bring the money?"

"No, but I'm good for it. I just don't know if they are going to go for it or not. Even though it's the truth."

"Look, that wasn't the deal. I did what you asked me to do. Now I want my money."

He laughed and said, "I'm going to give you the money."

"I suppose that Starr took you back?"

"Not yet."

"Do you think you two will be back together?"

He shrugged. "I don't know."

She stepped toward him and caressed his chest and they made eye contact. He leaned into her and kissed her. His hands gripped her firm little ass and she stepped back and dropped her pants. She was standing in the kitchen with a purple thong. His dick throbbed. She removed her blouse and her perky titties were now staring at him.

She said, "I need some right now, Q."

His eyes gave her a once over. She licked her lips. She inched toward him and stood on her tiptoes and kissed him again. His hands were right above her ass crack. He dropped his pants and then his underwear and she fondled his balls.

"You miss me?" she asked.

"I did."

She turned and spread her legs, her ass now facing him. "Penetrate me right fucking now."

He approached her and his dick was now rigid with pre-cum seeping from it.

She said, "Fuck me, Q."

He took a deep breath and said, "My God! What am I doing?"

He stepped back and picked his underwear up from the floor and slid into them. "I'll give you the seventy-five thousand dollars by the end of the week. I can't do this. I'm trying to be better."

She picked her jeans up from the floor and said, "Get the fuck out."

*****

Big Ced, Shamari, and TeTe's bodyguard Country sat at her kitchen table. TeTe revealed to Big Ced that he was going to be working for her from now on.

Big Ced rubbed his chin and said, "Don't you run a ho house?"

Everyone at the table laughed except TeTe.

"Do you want to get paid?"

"I do."

"Okay, I'm sure Shamari told you that I was the plug and I remember that you used to make money with Black and he thought a lot of you."

"He did and he thought a lot of you too. He'd told me that he'd never had a bitch like you."

"Nobody has."

"So you got product?"

"Yes."

"Like what? Ounces or kilos?"

"I got whatever the fuck you need."

"Do you know anything about the dope game?"

40

"I sold coke when your young ass was pissing on yourself."

Shamari said, "She's old school, but she knows what she is doing."

"You damn right I know what I'm doing."

The doorbell rang and TeTe came back into the room. There were two trannies and a girl who was clearly a call girl wearing a tight blue sequin dress and high heels.

Ced said, "Yo, what the fuck is going on in here?" He stood and was about to leave the kitchen. "Yo, I didn't sign up for this shit to be a part of a circus."

Fy-Head said, "Nigga, you're a motherfucking clown. So as far as I'm concerned, you're already part of a circus."

"I don't want to be around women dressing like niggas."

Shamari said, "You mean niggas dressing like women?"

Fy-Head said, "Who the hell is this cornball?"

TeTe stepped up to Ced and slapped the fuck out of him.

He snatched TeTe up by the blouse and pinned her narrow ass to the wall.

Her bodyguard Country rose to his feet and seized Big Ced and smashed his face hard on the hardwood floors and seizing his hand and cocked the coal black .380 and pressed it onto Ced's forehead.

TeTe screamed, "Don't do it."

Country kicked Ced 's ribcage and then eased the gun back into his pocket.

TeTe said, "Look, bruh, you can work with us or against us, but thought you wanted to get paid."

"I do."

Ced slowly rose to his feet then rolled his eyes. Fy-Head sat back at the table.

"What kind of weight you got?"

"Bricks."

"What's the price?"

"Thirty-six."

"I can get them for thirty-four."

"On consignment?"

"No."

"I'm going to front you whatever you need."

"That's cool. And I'll take what I can get right now. I'm fucked up." Ced cut his eyes at Fy-Head again.

Fy-Head said, "Ms. TeTe, if he looks at me like that one more time, it's going to be problems up in this motherfucka. I promise you that."

"There ain't going to be no problems nowhere. Ain't nobody starting shit up in here."

Ced said, "Why are they here in the first place?"

"They are here because they're my family and they are going to be the transporters."

Ced looked at Willow then winked. "I want baby girl to bring me my shit."

TeTe said, "It ain't about who or what you want. You're going to want whoever the fuck I tell to bring you your shit."

 Ced said, "So when do we get started. When can I get my first?"

*****

Fy-Head pulled out of the Super 8 parking lot. She'd been staying there since she was released from prison because she had nowhere else to go. She had called her mom the moment she got out and the conversation went like this.

"You ain't bringing your trifling ass and that goddamned freak show to my house."

"But Ma, I have nowhere else to go."

"Your problem, not mine."

"But I just got out, Ma. How you going to do me like this."

"This is the eighth time yo ass has gotten out of jail, or prison, or some other kind of institution. I can't do this no more, Casey. I'm getting too old to be worried about your bullshit."

"But Ma—"

"Don't come near my house or I'm going to call the police on your ass. Try me if you want to."

Dial Tone.

As Fy-Head recalled the conversation with her mother, she noticed a silver Nissan Murano with flashing blue lights behind her. She pulled over and two plainclothes cops approached. A white man and a black man, both in their mid-thirties. The black man was Barry Daniels, who had just returned to work after a month long investigation from Internal Affairs. The white man was David Lee, a friend of Daniels.

David Lee flashed his badge and said, "I'm with the FBI."

Fy-Head said, "FBI? What the fuck do y'all want from me?"

Barry Daniels bypassed David Lee and said, "Can we see your license and registration?"

Fy-Head presented him the license. Barry Daniels and David Lee looked at each other confused.

"This is a picture of a man."

"I was born a man."

"Casey King?"

"Yes, that's my name."

"You're transgender?"

"Yes. You couldn't tell?" Fy-Head asked and was actually proud of the way her make-up looked today. Most of the time, people would whisper that she was a man.

"Step out of the car, Casey."

Fy-Head stepped out of the car and when they saw the ginormous fake Louboutins that she was wearing, it was evident that Casey had been born a man.

Barry Daniels said, "I'm going to give you a chance to help us out and help yourself out without being charged."

"Being charged for what? Y'all bet' not put a hand on me either, or I'll make a scene out here. And you should be ashamed of yourself, sellout-ass nigga out here trying to impress the white man."

"Calm down."

"Calm down for what? I know my fucking rights."

An elderly white couple driving an old Chevy gave a glance in their direction and Fy-Head yelled, "They are harassing me. Record this shit. Black lives matter! #Translivesmatter."

The couple sped away and Fy-Head yelled, "Old racist crackers." Then she turned back to the agents.

"So what you pull me over for?"

Barry said, "Will you please calm down?"

"What did you pull me over for?"

"Can we talk for a second?"

"Talk about what?"

"Do you know Theresa Myers?"

"I don't know nobody by that name."

"TeTe."

"Okay, what do you want to know about her? If you trying to get me to say something about Ms. TeTe, you got the wrong one. Find yourself another snitch."

David Lee walked back to the car with Fy-Head's license still in his hand. He ran his name through NCIC, the National Crime Information Center, which was a database of criminal records.

Barry Daniels said, "We saw this car leaving TeTe's house last night."

"So what? It's not against the law to leave a friend's house."

"You know what line of work TeTe is in?"

"No, I don't know what she does. Why don't you tell me, Mr. FBI?"

David Lee approached Barry and Fy-Head then handed Fy-Head her license back.

Fy-Head said, "I don't know what she does."

"So are you one of her girls?"

"I'm nobody's girl. My status is HIV positive and I'm proud of it."

David Lee said, "You're out on bond for the murder of Dr. Craig Matthews."

Barry Daniels said, "You murdered Craig Matthews?"

"I plead the fifth."

"Interesting. So that means you know Shamari and you knew Black."

"I knew Black." Fy-Head had met Shamari but these nosy-ass cops didn't need to know that.

"Look, we've been trying to bring TeTe's agency down for a while. I need you to give me something on her and I'll let you go."

"Let me go? Motherfucker, you ain't got shit to hold me on."

"You like to shoplift? Take shit that don't belong to you? You have a long list of larcenies and shoplifting cases."

"What the fuck does that have to do with anything?"

"If I search this car, you're telling me I won't find any stolen goods?"

"Search the motherfucka if that's what you want to do."

David Lee and Barry Daniels rummaged through the car, looking under the seat and in the glove compartment, the armrest, and finally in the trunk. Fy-Head stood with her hands on her hips but they couldn't find anything. David Lee "You are free to go."

Fy-Head said, "Fuck the police."

Barry Daniels said, "Wait a minute. Let me see what's in that purse."

"I ain't letting you see shit. You've searched the car."

Fy-Head struck out running, yelling, "Black lives matter. Trans lives matter."

Barry Daniels tackled her ass and wrestled the purse away from her. Fy-Head grabbed his legs and that's when David Lee kicked the fuck out of her.

 Fy-Head yelled, "Get your cameras! Get your camera phone! They are trying to kill a bitch!"

 Barry Daniels opened the purse and spotted a ziplock bag filled with a powdery substance of what looked to be pure cocaine.

"What is this?"

"Sugar? Flour? I don't know what the fuck it is. I don't know how it got there. Did you put it there? You done went and planted some shit on me."

David Lee cuffed Fy-Head's ass, picked her up, and slammed her against the car.

"You're a drug dealer?"

"Yes."

"You're lying."

"If you think I'm lying, why did you ask me this?"

"This shit belongs to TeTe, right?"

"No."

 Barry Daniels said, "Put her ass in the car and we're going downtown."

They took Fy-Head to an office warehouse building.

"This don't look like no goddamned police station."

"That's because it ain't."

David Lee and Daniels carried Fy-Head inside the building and locked her up inside of a steel cage. Then they put a bag of dry cereal and water inside.

"You ain't no real FBI."

Daniels said, "You need to shut the hell up or else."

"Or else what?"

"Or else I'll kill your ass."

"If I don't get my meds, I'm going to die anyways. And I might be going to prison for murder. Do you think I give a fuck about dying? I damn sure don't give a fuck about going to prison. I'm a fag. You know what that means? Bitch, I'm like Amber Rose on a prison yard. Every motherfucker in there want to fuck me and don't give a fuck about my status."

 Barry Daniels laughed "Who did you get the coke from?"

Fy-Head sat in the middle of the floor.

"Look, I ain't got shit to say to you. I don't know who the fuck you are with those fake-ass badges. You can just leave me the fuck alone."

TeTe stepped out of the drycleaners and hung her clothes in the backseat of the Tesla.

"Excuse me, Theresa."

TeTe turned in a hurry. Nobody called her by her real name. When she turned, there was a goddamned FBI agent. She stepped toward him and asked, "What do you want with me?"

"Just wanted to know how the coke business is going?"

"I don't know anything about the coke business."

"Let's not play games. You're in the coke business and I'm in the protection business."

TeTe tried her best to figure out how in the hell he'd gotten this information. How in the hell did he know she was in the drug business? She hadn't been in business but a week and the Feds were onto her ass. Maybe it was her phone. Maybe it was someone in her circle. She had to find out where the leak was coming from.

"Let me help you."

"Help me do what?"

"Stop any investigation that might be going on with you."

"If anybody is investigating me, it's for hoes not dope."

He narrowed his eyes. "Why don't you cut the bullshit, TeTe? You're in the coke business and I can help. I need ten percent of your profits for protection."

"I don't sell dope."

"Yes, you do. I know that for a fact."

"And how do you know that?"

He flashed Fy-Head's license.

"She told you that?"

"Actually he didn't or wouldn't tell me a thing. You have a real solider on your hands."

"Where is she?"

"You mean he?"

"You know what the fuck I mean."

"He's in a safe place. Twenty-five thousand dollars and I'll let him go."

"Fuck you!"

 He passed her a card and she refused it.

"I have one already."

"This is a new one."

She took the card and tossed it into her purse.

*****

Jada and Shantelle met up for drinks at Halo Lounge on West Peachtree. This had been the first time that she'd seen Shantelle since she had exchanged cars with her in Alabama to enable Fresh's product to arrive to Atlanta.

Shantelle said, "Jada, girl, what the hell happened that night that you met me in Alabama? What was that about?"

"The short version of the story is this crooked-ass police had some information on me that I didn't want to get out and he wanted me to actually let him know when the product was coming in so he could take it. He wasn't going to arrest anyone. He just wanted to take the product to put on the street."

"Damn. So you tricked him?"

"I didn't have a choice. Look, I don't know how you were raised but me and Starr, we're street girls. Grew up in the hood. Starr was lucky because her daddy hustled. I didn't know my daddy, but the one thing about being in the streets is that you don't cross a motherfucka' that has been good to you and as trifling as Fresh is, he has been good to me."

"I understand."

"Do you really?"

"Yes. As a matter of fact, I just did a favor for Q the other day."

"Well, I certainly hope you didn't fuck the man again."

"What?" Shantelle was surprised at Jada's candidness, but she shouldn't have been; she knew that Jada's loyalty was with Starr.

"What happened?"

"I don't know if I told you or not, but Q didn't have Trey killed. It was a guy named Monte who had been texting Trey's crazy baby mama encouraging her to take Trey out."

"How did you find this out?"

"Q's attorney found it out indirectly."

"What do you mean, he found it out indirectly, and how did you get the information from Q?"

Shantelle could see where the conversation was going. "Q came over the other day."

"For what?"

"He wanted a favor."

"And why would he want you to do him a favor after he tried to kill you? Or at least that's what you said."

"That's what happened. Can I please explain myself? This is not a situation where I was trying to fuck Q," Shantelle said, though she did fuck him, but she damn sure wasn't about to tell Jada.

Jada said, "Okay, I won't cut you off."

"After he found out the information about Monte. He wanted me to go to the cops and tell them what I knew about Monte. He wanted me to tell them that it was Monte and not him that was texting Trey's baby mama."

"And you did this for him?"

"I did. I didn't want to do it, but I did it."

"And so what is going to happen next?"

"I don't know, but I didn't want to do it."

"So why did you do it?"

"Because he promised that he would help me. He said he would give me seventy-five thousand dollars to open up a studio."

"And you believe him?"

"Yes."

"You did the right thing."

"I did? I snitched, Jada. I snitched on Monte and you didn't snitch. You tricked the Feds so they wouldn't get Fresh's product and you covered up for Fresh."

"Q was going to probably go away for a long time if you didn't say something. Go away for something that he didn't do. In this game, doing the right thing is not always black and white."

"Why didn't he do it himself?"

"He's a gangsta. A gangsta would never sit down with the police, but he needed you to do it and you did it."

"I guess."

"Don't be so hard on yourself. You're a down-ass chick."

Later that night, Jada and Shantelle went back to Jada's place. They sat in her living room watching the new TV series ATLANTA, drinking Moscato. After three drinks Shantelle massaged Jada's thigh lightly and Jada didn't move her hand. Jada removed her jeans and then her panties. Shantelle stood and removed her leggings and stripped down to a tiny white thong revealing her long lean legs and well defined glutes. She inched forward and they locked lips. Jada's hand was now on Shantelle's ass and it was surprisingly soft. She'd always imagined that all of those workout bitches on Instagram had strong, manly asses. Shantelle was not her type at all. She preferred curvier women.

Jada led her to her bedroom. Jada dove into the bed and laid on her back and spread her legs. Jada was known to please women orally sometimes, but not often. Shantelle crawled into the bed with Jada and they kissed. Jada slid Shantelle's underwear down and inserted her index finger inside Shantelle's love hole. Shantelle was already wet and this aroused Jada. Jada leaned over then took possession Shantelle's breast. She had just a mouthful.

Shantelle whispered, "You're a selfish lover, aren't you?"

"I am."

Shantelle laughed. The Moscato on her breath assaulted Jada's nostrils.

She said, "Hey, it's okay. I'm a pleaser and I like you. I've always thought you were the sexiest of your three friends."

"Yeah?"

"Yeah."

"Even after I beat your ass?" Jada said. Then she laughed and said, "I'm sorry."

"Yeah, even after you beat my ass."

Jada forced Shantelle's head down to her navel ring. Shantelle's tongue now tracing Jada's navel.

"Lick my clit," Jada ordered.

Shantelle giggled and said, "You're so damn bossy."

This bitch was turning Jada off and Jada was about to tell her to just get the fuck up and go, then Shantelle's tongue brushed her clit and then her mouth covered her labia. And Jada held her pillow tight.

Shantelle kept licking and sucking until she found the spot.

"Right there." Jada's eyes widened as she clenched the pillow. "Keep going."

Shantelle eased her finger inside Jada's opening and Jada said, "Push it deeper."

And Shantelle obliged, pushing her finger deeper while nibbling on her clit. With blood hurrying to the tip of Jada's clit, she hadn't felt this good in a long time. No man knew what to do with her clit like Shantelle.

Jada could feel Shantelle ease up. Jada forced her head back down and Shantelle kept going until Jada erupted and she shivered and convulsed. Shantelle climbed up to the head of the bed and Jada was still lying there with her eyes closed, not knowing what to believe. All she knew right now was that this girl lying beside her had given her an incredible orgasm. One like she'd never experienced with a man. She opened her eyes and found Shantelle staring at her, smiling.

"I never would have thought you were into girls."

"I have a time or two, but it's not really my thing."

"Mine either. I'm like you. I've been with a few women. Did you like it?"

Jada smiled brightly then covered her face with the pillow and said, "Girl, you don't even want to know."

Shantelle tried to pluck the pillow from Jada's hand and said, "I do want to know."

Jada removed the pillow from her face and said, "You were unbelievable."

"Thank you."

"No one can find out about this."

"Of course not."

Jada smiled.

"You're afraid I will tell Starr?" Shantelle said. "Wait a minute, have you and Starr—"

Jada cut her off. "Starr is straight laced, and for the record, she knows I'll do a girl when I get the notion to."

"So who don't you want to know?"

"You know sometimes when word gets back to guys, they can't handle it. Every man I've been with knows that I'm bi, but you know how men are as long as you are with them, it's okay, but you do something when they ain't around, it's a problem."

They laughed and then Shantelle took Jada's hand and locked her fingers with Jada's hands and then leaned into her and they kissed again.

Jada said, "Have you ever been in a relationship with a girl?"

Shantelle stared at the ceiling and said, "You know when I was seventeen, I had a friend named Aria that I used to be on the tennis team with. We were the only two black girls on the team and we used to hookup all the time. We were together but we both had boyfriends that had no idea that we were into girls."

"Aria was her name?"

"Yes."

"I like that name."

"Me too."

Jada was thinking that her and Shantelle had nothing in common. She was from a world of girl names like Aria and Caitlin that played tennis and swam and Jada was from a world of girl names like Starr and Meeka. But this girl Shantelle had made her feel great.

"Yeah, I used to hook up with a chick when I was in high school too."

"Am I your type?"

Jada covered her face with the pillow again and said. "OMG."

"I guess not, huh?"

She removed the pillow and said, "To keep it real with you, no you're not my type. I generally like a softer, curvier female. Don't get me wrong. I like your body and I know you put a lot of work into it, but it's just not something I like, but I swear the way you work that tongue I might have to reconsider. So how did you start liking D-Boys, Shantelle? You know you really don't seem like the type."

"I know."

"Tell me about it."

"When I lived in Washington I was dating this guy named Josh that I'd met at the gym and he had plants in his basement. I didn't really think nothing of it. I was like it's only weed and then he'd started traveling the world that I'd only dreamed of."

"Where did y'all go?"

"We'd went to South of France and Venice, Italy and it was really fun. Then one day, Feds busted his house and confiscated over a million dollars in cash and that's when I learned that he was big time. He went away for a while. I moved to Atlanta and I was just drawn to the guys with the money. I guess you could say that he spoiled me."

"But you have a college degree."

"What the hell does that mean? I wanted the American dream just like everybody else."

"I don't want you to be a courier again."

"I never planned on being a courier, but a girl has to do what a girl has to do."

"I understand."

There was a really awkward silence and Shantelle said, "I really like you, Jada."

"I like you too."

"I don't think you understand what I'm saying, Jada."

"What are you saying?"

"I want to be with you."

"Whoa."

"I'm serious."

"Okay."

"You don't feel the same way?"

"I don't know what I feel."

Jada leaned into Shantelle and locked lips.

*****

Diamond Princess and Willow had inquired about Fy-Head and they seemed to be very concerned about her. They kept asking TeTe if she had heard from her. They knew that the last time they had seen her, she was supposed to deliver some product in the hood to Big Ced. Diamond Princess swore to God that if she found out that Big Ced had harmed her sister in anyway, she was going to kill his ass.

TeTe said, "Calm down. I spoke with her and she's fine."

"That bitch answered your calls and not mine?" Diamond Princess said.

"Look, she wanted to make some extra money so I sent her to South Carolina," TeTe lied.

"She ain't tell me."

"She don't need to tell you everything, does she?"

"I tell her everything."

TeTe said, "Look, I need you to take Ced some product."

"You know he don't like me."

TeTe turned to Willow and said, "Can you do it for me?"

"Of course."

"Look, this is different. If you get caught with this shit, you're going to prison for a long time."

Diamond Princess said, "I'll take it."

TeTe said, "Yeah, I want Diamond to take it and you can come with me."

"Where are we going?'

TeTe said, "Can you quit asking so many goddamned questions?"

Willow smiled.

TeTe trotted upstairs to get the product for Big Ced. She passed it to Diamond Princess in a Nordstrom's shopping bag and TeTe and Willow climbed into her Range Rover and hit 285 to Sandy Springs. They pulled over at a Waffle House and they went inside and ordered some pecan waffles. Twenty minutes later, Stunna drove up. He climbed out of the car and looked both ways.

Willow, who was sitting on the same side of the booth as TeTe, spreading grape jam on wheat toast, said, "Is that man driving the Maserati coming to see you?"

"Yes, why?"

"I've never seen a man that gorgeous in my whole life, and I've never really liked black men."

"You need to come out of that damn trailer park and live life a little more. There's more to life than drunk rednecks named Dylan wearing ripped jeans watching NASCAR."

Willow was laughing her ass off when Stunna approached the table.

He slid into the booth and then he looked at Willow and smiled. He extended his hand. "What's your name, l'il mama?"

Willow's panties were moist. She would lay her ass across the table and fuck this tall dark handsome specimen right here in the Waffle House. All he had to do was ask and the pussy was his on a platter.

She said, "My name is Willow."

"Beautiful girl." He winked.

Willow blushed.

TeTe said, "Look, can we cut the flirting and can we get down to business?"

"Okay, what did you want to talk to me about that you couldn't talk about on the phone?"

"I got what you need."

Stunna frowned. He narrowed his eyes and focused his gaze on Willow to let TeTe know he was uncomfortable talking about any kind of business in front of Willow. And as far as he knew, TeTe was a madam and not a drug dealer.

"Look, Stunna, I know you're surprised."

"I don't know what you're talking about?"

"Cut the bullshit."

TeTe called Shamari and passed Stunna the phone.

"Shamari, I'm here with TeTe and she's trying to—"

Shamari cut him off. "TeTe is the plug now."

Stunna laughed.

"Seriously, bruh. You know she was Black's old lady before he died. She's cool. Trust me."

"Aight, call me later." He ended the call.

"Okay, you have what I want?"

"I do."

Stunna glanced at Willow. She nibbled on wheat toast with grape jam. He'd imagined her pretty little mouth wrapped around his dick. "Who are you again?"

"Willow."

"And is it necessary for Willow to be here?" He cut his eyes to her and said, "No offense, Willow, I'm sure you're cool, but we're about to discuss some business. You know what I mean?"

"She's one of my girls, but I can get her to change tables if it will make you more comfortable."

"No, it's okay. If you say it's okay for her to stay, who am I to tell her to leave?"

Willow smiled.

Stunna said, "So you got what I want?"

"Yes, of course."

"What is it that I want?"

"Raw."

"I have a connect already."

"But you don't have a price like mine."

"Oh yeah?"

"What are you paying right now?"

"Right now, I'm paying twenty-eight."

"I'll give it to you for twenty-six and that's your price only, I'm charging everyone else between thirty-four to thirty six."

"But is it any good?"

"The best."

"There is only one problem."

TeTe narrowed her eyes. "What problem?"

"I don't do business with women unless you're in my family. I have a different breed of women in my family."

"And what breed is that?"

"Gangsta."

TeTe laughed and said, "You have no idea who the fuck you're talking to." TeTe was used to men underestimating her.

"Look, TeTe, thanks but I'm good. I'm really good right now." He stood and was walking toward the door. TeTe followed him out into the parking lot. Stunna sat on the Maserati hood. Willow was still inside the Waffle House.

TeTe said, "Look, can you just think about it?"

"Why do you want me on your team so bad?"

"Because you can move a ton of product. No other reason."

"If I do decide to, can you give it to Shamari and I get it from him?"

"Whatever makes you feel better. I just need you to be down with me."

"I'll think about it. I can't make any promises. Things are going well right now." He looked through the window at Willow who was still eating. He made eye contact with her and she smiled and he said, "Is she really one of your girls?"

"Yes. You want her?"

"She's pretty."

"I thought you were talking to Jada's friend. What's her name?"

"Starr?"

"Yeah, Starr. I met her a few times. Seemed like a nice girl."

"Yeah." He sighed. "That's over."

"Sorry to hear that. But if you want Willow, I'll send her over tonight."

"How much?"

TeTe grinned. "It's on the house."

He smiled and TeTe realized that there was a gold grill on his bottom row of teeth. Sexy motherfucker. She thought to herself.

He said, "TeTe, I hope you don't think that this is going to influence me to work with you."

"Not at all. It's a friend doing another friend a favor."

"Send her over."

"Think about what I said."

Later at TeTe's, Diamond Princess called informing her that she'd dropped the product off with Big Ced. Then she asked how was Fy-Head doing. TeTe assured her that she was doing fine, but TeTe didn't know that for sure. She dialed Barry Daniels number.

"Hello?"

"Look, I need you to release Cassandra. I mean Casey."

"Well, you know what you have to do."

"How do I know that you're going to do what you said you would do?"

"Look, I'll let her go right now. I don't need you to give me anything. I'll take your word that you're going to pay your debt. But if you don't ..."

"If I don't? What are you going to do?"

"Ask Black. Oh, you can't ask Black, can you?"

TeTe felt an emptiness when he said that. Daniels was heartless.

"Let her go then."

"Okay, I'm going to do better than that. I'll let her go and I'll return the product. Just make sure I get what I asked for."

"You'll get your money."

 She ended the call.

The phone rang. It was Diamond Princess again. "What is going on?"

"What do you mean what's going on? You called me a few minutes ago and I told you that she was doing fine."

"It's been four days and I have not heard from my friend."

"I told you she was handling business for me."

"Look, Ms. TeTe, I'm giving you by the end of the week and if somebody don't tell me what the fuck is going on with my friend, somebody is going to get fucked up."

TeTe stared at the phone and realized that this little tranny ho really didn't know who she was talking to. She wanted to curse her the fuck out then go to her house and drag her outside and toss her ass in a lake, or push her in front of an eighteen-wheeler or dangle her ass over a ledge. But she just kept her calm. Clearly the ho didn't know who the fuck she was talking to.

"Did you hear me, Ms. TeTe?"

"Yes I heard you, but I surely hope this is not a threat."

She began to sob. "I'm sorry, Ms. TeTe. I know you're crazy. I know that you'll kill me. I was just thinking out loud. This is my best friend and I don't know what I'll do without her."

"I get that and I'm sorry that it's taken this long, but we had a situation. I swear to you she's fine."

"I'm relieved. I believe you."

"Diamond?"

"Yes."

"We're going to forget that this conversation ever happened, but I swear to you, if you ever threaten me again, I'll kill your little ass. Is that understood?"

There was silence on the other end of the phone.

"Is that understood?"

"Yeah and I'm sorry."

"As a matter of fact, if you tell somebody that this conversation took place, you're a dead man, understand?"

"I'm a woman."

"Whatever the fuck you are, it won't matter anyway because you'll be dead. A dead man, a dead woman, or a dead tranny bitch. You'll be dead. Don't ever fucking threaten me again."

"Look, I understand."

Two hours had gone by and TeTe was lying on the sofa watching 60 MINUTES when the doorbell rang. She ran to the door and opened it. It was Fy-Head. She was standing there with matted weave and parched lips. She looked a lot thinner.

TeTe invited her in.

Fy-Head rummaged through her purse and handed TeTe the coke. "You'll never guess what happened. I know you probably thought that I took your shit, but I didn't. I still have everything. I got pulled over by two guys that said they were FBI and they took me to a warehouse and locked me in this steel cage and fed me dry cereal for four fucking days."

"Stop. I already know about all of this."

"You do?" Her voice rose a couple of octaves.

"I spoke to the guy already and he agreed to let you go, but I have to pay him."

"Who the fuck is that asshole? 'Tombout he the FBI."

"Well, he is."

"He is?"

"Yeah, but he wants to get paid. Wants me to pay him."

"What the fuck?"

"Yeah."

Fy-Head said, "Can I take a shower? I've had this shit on for four days."

"Go through those double doors and there is a walk-in shower in the bathroom on the right. I'll get some shorts and some sweatpants for you to put on, though I don't know if you can stuff all that ass in my sweatpants."

Fy-Head said, "Girl, you a mess." Then she stopped and started twerking. "It is big, ain't it?"

"Your little friend Diamond been calling every five minutes."

"I know she's worried."

"Look, I want you to have a talk with her."

"About what?"

"You need to tell her that I'm the wrong one to fuck with."

"What does that mean? What did she do?"

"Just do what I say."

"Anything for you, Ms. TeTe. And I want you to know that I didn't say shit to them about you. I never admitted to anything."

"I know and I love you for that."

Fy-Head was walking in the direction of the bathroom when she stopped and said, "Ms. TeTe, what are we going to do?"

TeTe made eye contact with her and said, "I don't know. I don't know."

*****

It was 9:15 p.m. and John was sipping hot green tea as he wound down for bed, when he heard a knock on his door. He ran to the door and opened it to find TeTe standing there. He invited her in.

He said, "Excuse my ugly green pajamas, but I wasn't expecting company."

TeTe ignored his ass. She could care less about his pajamas. She knew she was too old for John. He was too corny for her, but she needed his corny ass right now. She marched right pass him and sat down on a sofa. He followed her. He sat beside her and he offered her tea and she declined and thought who the fuck sips tea in ugly green pajamas at night. Lonely corny motherfuckers was her guess.

"Okay, what's wrong?" he asked. He sipped his tea.

"We have to kill the FBI agent."

He chuckled and said, "What do you mean we?"

"Look, I mean me. I have to kill him. We have to knock his ass off, John. There is no other way around it. He's making my life a living hell."

"TeTe, you're the one that talked Stunna out of killing him. What the hell has gotten into you? I've known you for a long time and I've gone in and cleaned up a lot of murder scenes for you, but you have no idea the kind of heat killing a Fed agent brings."

TeTe rubbed her chin. She did actually know. She'd actually killed two DEA agents in South Carolina many years ago and she did

70

know that this would bring heat, but it was heat that she was willing to deal with. She had to get rid of this agent Barry Daniels.

"What can I do then?"

"Maybe I can contact my friends to get some dirt on him."

"Please get some dirt on him."

"What happened?"

"I don't want to talk about it."

"Tell me."

"I'm in the coke business now."

"What? Why? You know this is going to end up bad. You know it's going to end up with you going to prison for a long time."

 She dropped her head and said, "I know but after that goddamned football player OD'd, TMZ has been set up outside my house for the last two weeks. I couldn't operate. Everybody is saying I'm the madam that sent the girls up to his room. So they've been all over my ass."

"So you decide to sell coke?" John said. "You think that's going to bring less heat? That's going to bring more heat to your ass if somebody gets caught and it seems like you couldn't be doing a good job at it because the Feds are already on your ass."

TeTe buried her face inside the palms of her hands. "I know."

"How did that happen?"

"It's a long story and I don't want to talk about it."

"I ain't got nothing but time."

"Apparently he'd been watching my house and he followed one of my workers. She gets pulled over and has coke that she was supposed to deliver for me."

"Deliver? So he took her to jail?"

"No. He didn't arrest her."

"I don't understand."

"He just held her for collateral to let me know he knows what I'm up to and he doesn't give a damn that I operate. He just wants ten percent."

"Give it to him."

"Hell, no. I don't trust him. Something is going on with his guy. I want to kill him. We got to kill him. That's the only option."

"Let me try to get some dirt on him because if you think you have problems now, just wait until you kill a federal agent.

*****

Stunna strolled around his condo shirtless, revealing his chiseled abdomen. He hardly worked out, but he was one of those black men who were genetically gifted and no matter what he ate, he'd never gain weight. Willow sat on the sofa with her eyes on Stunna's sexy, coal-colored body. She wanted to fuck the man and she'd fuck him for free even though TeTe had promised her a couple of thousand dollars for the job.

He turned and made eye contact with her and smiled. "Why are you looking at me like that?"

"Like what?"

 He smiled revealing just one dimple on his left cheek. "I can't describe it, but you are looking at me like You've never seen a man before."

"Look, Stunna, I don't know how much TeTe told you about me."

"She didn't tell me anything about you."

"I'm biracial."

"I can see that. She didn't have to tell me that." He laughed.

She laughed and said, "I know you can see that, smartass."

"Tell me about you."

"I grew up around white people. My first boyfriend was white. My second boyfriend was white. My third boyfriend was white."

"Whoa. Are you saying that you don't like black guys? Hey, if that's the case, it's cool with me. You don't have to go through with it."

"That's not what I'm saying at all. I think you're the most beautiful man I've seen in my life."

"I don't think I've heard anyone describe me as beautiful."

"Do you have a girlfriend?"

"No, What about you?"

"I don't have a girlfriend."

"You know what I meant."

"No, I don't have a man."

"Have you ever been with a black man?"

"I have, but not as his girlfriend."

"How old are you, Willow?"

"Twenty-two."

"You're young. I don't usually fuck with young girls."

"And you're about thirty."

"Close. How old are you, again?"

"Does it matter?"

"Look, I don't want to feel like I'm robbing the cradle."

"I'm a grown woman."

"Have you met TeTe's friend John?"

"OMG, he's such a perv."

Stunna laughed. This girl clearly had been around white people most of her days.

"I met TeTe through John. I used to have an ad on Backpage and he called me one night and the next morning TeTe came over."

"Damn, you're honest and open about what you do."

"That's the only way I know to be. I find when you are honest, people can't do shit to you and hold it against you. You know what I mean?"

Stunna phone buzzed. It was a text from the UPS driver B.C. HEY, DID YOU FORGET ABOUT THE BOX? IT CAME TODAY.

Stunna excused himself and called Micky. The call went straight to voice mail.

He entered back in the room and Willow was undressed. She was so pretty. Her body was lean like a flat-chested ballerina. Not quite what Stunna was used to. She approached him with child-like innocence and massaged his chest.

He kissed her once then said, "Put you clothes back on."

She pressed her lips tight then frowned.

"You're too young," Stunna said.

"I'm twenty-two."

"Like I said, you're not a woman. If you were twenty-two and your body was voluptuous, nothing would stop me from fucking you, but you're built like a kid."

 Willow slid back into her clothes.

 She removed her phone from her purse and said, "My battery died. Can you call me an Uber?"

"You don't have a car?"

"It's in the shop."

"Where are you going?"

"I'm going to Marietta_ _ _ _"

"I'll take you there. I have to make a stop first."

"Okay, fine and I appreciate the ride."

"No problem."

They jumped into Stunna's F150 and hit the highway. They pulled into B.C.'s sub division and B.C. came out and tossed a box onto the back of the cab. Stunna handed him a wad of hundred dollar bills.

The UPS driver said, "See you again next Wednesday." Then he disappeared into his apartment.

When they drove away, Willow said, "Was that your plug?"

Stunna looked at the naive little trailer park bitch and said, "What do you know about a plug?"

"I've heard it in a song." She laughed.

"Do you know what a plug is?"

"A plug is a connect."

"I thought you said you were from a trailer park."

"I am but my dad sold meth."

Stunna said, "No, that was not my plug. There was an awkward silence then he unzipped his pants and removed his tool, and guided her head into the direction of his dick. She just stared at the sheer size of his ginormous long, thick, rigid tool. She took him in her mouth and pleasured him until he erupted into her pretty little mouth, just like he'd fantasized the first time he saw her at the Waffle House. Mission complete.

Starr embraced Q when he entered her home then she stared in his eyes for a very long time. She had missed him, and she was happy that he didn't have anything to do with Jessica's decision to kill Trey.

He said, "Damn, girl, I didn't know you were so strong."

She released him and said, "Speaking of strong. So you slept with Shantelle too, huh?"

"I did, but that was before I even moved to Atlanta."

"I know. She told me the whole story. That girl wants to fuck everybody that I've ever been with."

Q laughed and they entered the living room.

"Where is my man T.J.?"

"At my parent's house."

"I didn't know how much I missed that boy until I saw him the other day."

"What about your own kids. Do you ever miss them?"

"All the time. Why do you ask?"

"I never hear you talk about them?"

"Well, recently I've been fighting this case and didn't want to bother them, but I miss them and I want to move them to Atlanta."

"To live with you?"

"With their mother and her husband. I want to just get them a house so they will be near. I'll pay the mortgage, of course."

"You'll pay for the kid's mother and her man?"

"Why wouldn't I? I have the money and it's over between us. We've both moved on. My kids have a really nice step-father."

"You're a special man indeed."

"I'm a grown man. Would I have done this twenty years ago? Hell, no. I would have been another one of those lame-ass dudes starting trouble with my kid's mother—'tombout not wanting another man around the kids, knowing damn well that they are still in love with the woman."

Starr was laughing her ass off then she stopped and her forehead wrinkled.

"What's wrong?" he asked.

"Nothing."

"Uh-oh, I know better than that. When a woman says nothing, you better believe it's something."

"Well, I was just thinking about the baby I lost."

"Our baby...you mean."

"Q, you know you weren't the father of that child."

"But I was serious when I said I was going to help you raise it."

She smiled. She couldn't help but love this man.

He grabbed her hand and held it for a while. "Don't worry. I plan for us to have more. T.J. will have lots of brothers and sisters."

She kissed his hand and held onto it.

"Soon as I beat this case, I'm out of the game."

"You don't have to do that. Look, I've now realized I like what I like and I don't want you to be someone that you don't want to be."

"I have enough money. And I don't want to end up like Black or Fresh."

"What will you do?"

"Property investment, I guess because I'm selling all my businesses in Houston. I was thinking of opening up a few dry cleaners."

"Awesome."

"I think I'm going to buy a building, put the cleaners there and a check cashing business. Perhaps a UPS package store."

"You're so smart."

 "We'll see if it works."

"I'm sure it will." Then she kissed him and said, "I have a question for you."

"What?"

"Who bonded you out?"

"Fresh has a cousin here. He convinced him to bond me out." Q lied. He wasn't going to let Starr know that Meeka had in fact bonded him out.

*****

Jada pulled into the parking lot beside Gladys Knight's Chicken and Waffles then paid the attendant. She hopped out of her car and climbed into the passenger side of TeTe's Tesla.

Jada gave her a bright smile.

79

"What's up?"

"Man, I'm so stressed out."

"Stressed about what?"

"Barry Daniels, chile."

Jada was surprised. The last time she'd seen Barry Daniels, the Feds were hauling him away in a van.

"What about Barry Daniels?"

"He threatened me. He found out that I was dealing and he wants ten percent of everything that I make."

"What? Are you sure it was Barry Daniels?"

"Yes. Why don't you believe me?"

"Because a few weeks ago he threatened me and told me that if I didn't let him know when Fresh was bringing back product, he was going to get me for conspiracy. So my attorney set up a sting where I was supposed to bring back product and Barry was supposed to confiscate it. They were trying to bring him down."

"Well, obviously it didn't work."

Jada shot a blank stare and she was terrified that he was not in custody and that he was obviously still with the FBI.

"I need to tell you something," Jada said.

"Tell me."

"He killed Black."

"How do you know?"

"Because when I denied I had anything to do with the drug game, he showed me Black's phone. Shown me a text that I sent saying that I would keep some work at my house for him." Jada lied. She didn't want TeTe to know what the text really said, nor did she want TeTe to know that she'd fucked Black before he had died.

"Really?"

"Yes, I believe he killed Black. He killed him. I'm sure but I can't prove it. But why else would he have Black's phone?"

"Good point," TeTe said.

Jada glanced at her watch and said, "I have to go." And she gave TeTe a hug and climbed out of the car.

*****

Shamari invited TeTe into his home. Ava was strolling around in blue booty shorts. She held onto a folded slice of pepperoni pizza.

TeTe smiled at Ava. "Damn, Shamari got that ass looking fat. When do you want to come back to work for me?"

 Shamari shot TeTe a mean stare and she said, "Hey, man, I'm just playing. Can't you take a joke?" TeTe walked around the condo and said, "This is a really nice place you got here, Shamari."

"Yeah, I'm used to nice shit too." He pointed to the Papa John's pizza box and said, "Have a slice?"

"No thanks."

"What, you don't eat pork?"

"Nigga, I'm from South Carolina. I'll eat a chitlins pizza if you got one. But only in moderation."

81

Ava and Shamari laughed their asses off.

"So what brings you here?"

"It's Stunna."

"What about him?"

Ava beelined to Shamari's bedroom.

"What about Stunna?" Shamari asked again.

"He's not down with the program. He says he has his own connect and bullshit about he don't like doin' deals with women. I even offered him the work at two thousand dollars less than his plug."

"That's too bad. I served him but, I knew he had his own plug."

"Does he move a lot of work?"

"He does. I've never seen nothing like that in my life. There was only one person I ever seen move product like he does and that was Black."

"We need him."

"I know, right?"

"I'm wondering how much work he's buying."

"I don't know, but the man runs through the shit. I wouldn't be surprised if he's not buying at least twenty."

"I have to get him on our side."

Frank Ocean's NIKE played though a wooden speaker. Jada and Shantelle lay underneath the thick blue comforter staring at one another when the doorbell rang.

Shantelle said, "You expecting company?"

"No."

Jada climbed out of the bed and slid into a pair of tight, blue gym shorts. She then grabbed her iPhone and opened her security app to see who was at the door. It was Shamari. She dashed into the living room and opened the door. He whisked right past her without being invited in. She closed the door and turned and faced him. His eyes dropped to her breasts.

"Where is your bra?"

"You know I sleep naked." She yawned. "Shamari, it's early. What the hell do you want?"

"I just came to bring you the money that you paid the attorney for me. I just realized that I didn't pay you back."

"You didn't have to do that. I knew you were going to pay me."

"I was on my way to Carolina and that actually reminded me that I needed to pay you because I was going out of town the last time that you had given me the money."

"I remember."

He passed her a manila envelope stuffed full of bills.

He spotted a Louis Vuitton purse on the table, a pair of pink Nike running shoes and a Hello Kitty key chain.

"You have company?"

"My girlfriend spent the night."

"Where is she?"

"She's in the bed sleeping. Why?"

He looked surprised. "Y'all slept together?"

"Yes, we slept in the same bed. Girls can do that, you know?"

"I didn't mean it like that. I meant did you fuck? Make love?"

"No."

"Sure?"

"We didn't, but what difference does it make? You have someone."

Shantelle entered the room fully dressed in tight pink gym leggings and a T-shirt. "Calm down. Shamari, Me and Jada ain't bumping coochies. We had some drinks and I fell asleep over here. I didn't want to drive home and Jada said I could sleep in the bed with her."

"That's your business, shawty." Shamari made eye contact with Jada. "I just came to drop off the money."

She thanked him and he turned and walked away. After the door closed, Shantelle leaned into Jada and they locked lips.

"How long are we going to keep this a secret?" Shantelle asked.

"I don't know?"

"What do you mean, you don't know?"

"I don't know if I'm ready for everybody to know my business."

"Everybody means Shamari?"

"Yes."

"Why? He has someone."

"Like I said, I don't know."

"You care about what he thinks?"

"I do. I care maybe too much."

*****

TeTe handed Willow fifteen hundred dollars in fifty and hundred dollar denominations for seeing Stunna and Willow said, "That might have been the easiest fifteen hundred dollars I made in my life."

"What do you mean?"

"He wanted a blow job."

"A blow job." TeTe laughed.

"What's so funny?"

"It's just that I haven't heard that word in a long time. Usually people just say he wanted head. A blow job sounds so nineteen eighties."

"I guess so," Willow said.

"So he wanted head?"

"Honestly, I can't even say that he wanted head. I think since I was there, he accepted it. I don't know if I can say that he wanted head."

"You sound disappointed."

"I wanted him inside me. He was so fucking huge. I've never seen a cock that big in my life."

TeTe laughed to herself at Willow referring to a dick as a cock but what did she expect from the girl—this was the same girl who referenced head as a blow job.

"I'm thankful for the opportunity that you have given me but I'm going to have to go back to working on Backpage. The money here was good when I first started but since you got into the coke business, I've been hurting."

"I know and I understand, but if you can just hang in there with me for a few more weeks, I have a few big money clients coming into town."

"What am I supposed to do until then?"

"Just don't go cheapen yourself by selling ass on Backpage."

"I have no choice. Rent is coming up."

TeTe knew that this girl had earned thousands of dollars since she'd began working but there was no use in asking where the money went. She knew that most hoes were terrible with money. TeTe said, "I have a question."

"What?"

"A few weeks ago, you had a client that had given you a lot of money to bring Ava to you."

"Rico Suave."

"Who?"

"Dildo man."

"Yes, him."

"What happened to that money?"

"I think I told you my Dad is in prison for selling meth?"

"Yes."

"I paid his attorney. We're trying to get his sentenced reduced."

"Okay, that explains why you're broke."

"Yes. I have real-life problems. I don't blow my money on clothes and bags. I have real responsibilities."

"I can respect that."

TeTe passed her two more thousand dollars and said, "This is an advance and I'll get the money back from you when the clients come into town."

She smiled and said, "Thank you."

"So what did you and Stunna do?"

"I gave him HEAD and that was it." She smiled.

"He didn't want to fuck?"

"He didn't and that was kind of disappointing because I REALLY wanted to fuck that man. Did you see how he was built? My God. He's so damn perfect."

Stunna was very attractive to TeTe, too. Not only for his looks but also for his earning potential.

"So he gave you head?" TeTe wanted to keep the bitch on the subject, she knew oftentimes girls rambled and never got to the point.

She laughed and said, "No, I gave him head."

"And that was it?"

"That was it."

"Start from the beginning."

"I caught an Uber over to his place because my car's in the shop."

"What the hell? Your car is in the shop?"

"I drive a piece of shit Camry and that's another reason I don't have any money."

"Camry's are good cars."

"I supposed mine was good at one time, but now I have over four hundred thousand miles on it."

"Get a new car."

"I did. I just got a 2016 Avalon I'm supposed to pick it up tomorrow.

"Okay, get back to the story. You arrived at his house in an Uber."

"Yeah and we were having a pretty good conversation. I was telling him how I had grown up in a trailer park."

"Would you quit telling people that you grew up in a trailer park and raised by rednecks! Nobody wants to hear that and if I was a man that would turn me off. Men are simple creatures. They want glamour, nice dresses, and sexy heels. They like fantasy. Not some trailer park hoe that drinks moonshine and hunts squirrels with a bow and arrow."

Willow laughed her ass off.

"Yeah, he asked me how old I was and when I told him, I think it somehow turned him off. He started feeling guilty and saying shit like I was too young for him and then he asked me if I knew John. I thought it was an odd question but I told him that John had connected me and you."

"So when did you give him head?" TeTe asked again, bringing the air-headed bitch back to subject.

"I gave him head after he picked up this box from this guy."

"A box from a guy? What kind of box and where did y'all go and why did he take you with him?"

"Because my phone died and I couldn't call an Uber and I didn't have my charger. So he offered to take me home but said first he had to go pick up something from somebody."

"What did he pick up?"

"I have no idea what was in the box, but the guy was some non-descriptive, skinny-ass dude."

"What do you mean non descriptive?"

"I mean he was the basic, brown-complexioned, black man. You know the kind of man that you can't pick out of a crowd. He was just that basic, but I do remember that he had a UPS uniform on and he came out to the truck, and threw a box on the back of the cab. and said that he would see him again next Wednesday night."

"Oh yeah and I asked Stunna was he the plug and he seemed a little shocked that I had asked him that."

TeTe laughed and then she said, "Do you remember where this UPS driver lived?"

"Oh yeah, I remember how to get here.

"Do you think you can show me where he lives?"

"Yes."

"You have his address?"

"No but I remember there was a really nice Porsche in his driveway.

"Show me how to get there."

*****

When Butterfly opened the door to push her bike outside to take a spin in the neighborhood, there was a strange man on the doorstep.

"What is your name, little girl?" Barry Daniels asked.

"Butterfly." Butterfly stepped back.

"You have a beautiful name and you're a pretty little girl. Did I scare you?"

"Yes, I thought you were a clown."

"A clown?"

"Yes, scary clowns have been snatching little kids up and taking them to a faraway land. Don't you watch the news?"

"No."

"Then you might be a clown."

"No, I'm not a clown. Where is your mother?"

"She's upstairs but she's going to be pissed that I'm standing here talking to a stranger."

"Pissed, huh? How old are you?" Daniels was startled that the child had used the word pissed. She'd been hanging around adults too much.

90

"I don't know you to be telling you my age. And you can't come in." She slammed the door so hard the whole house vibrated. TeTe appeared at the top of the stairwell.

"Butterfly, what the hell is going on?"

"I was about to go outside and ride my bike like you said I could. But there is a strange man standing on the doorstep and I knew you would be pissed if I kept talking to him."

"A strange man? What the hell are you talking about?" TeTe scampered downstairs and opened the door and was startled that it was Barry Daniels.

"What the fuck are you doing here?"

"I came to collect."

TeTe turned to Butterfly. "Go to your room."

"You said I could ride my bike."

"What the fuck did I just say?"

Butterfly dropped her bicycle then stormed around the corner into her room bawling.

 TeTe invited Barry Daniels in and once he was inside and the door was closed, she asked, "Why in the fuck did you show up at my house?"

"To pick up my money."

"I don't have any money here."

"I don't believe you."

"It's true."

"Have my money by the end of the day."

"You'll get your money."

"Did you think about what I asked?"

"Refresh my memory, please, sir."

"About you operating. I need ten percent of whatever you make."

"Okay, I'm only getting a kilo at a time."

"I don't believe you."

"I don't care what you believe."

"TeTe, I've let this little prostitution ring run for a long time and I know how much money you were making sending those chicks over to Dubai and Miami. I know you didn't leave that business to sell drugs. I want in on what you got going on. I can make your life easier."

"Look, why don't you find someone, like you found Black? Get them to sell your shit and leave me the fuck alone."

"I can't. It doesn't work anymore. Let me help you and you help me."

"How are you going to help me again? Refresh my memory."

"I'll offer protection and get rid of your rivals."

"Look, I'll think about it, but can you leave now?"

Butterfly came running into the room screaming. "Ma, my TV won't play."

Barry and TeTe locked eyes. "My money, by the end of the day and think about what I said. You won't be able to operate if I don't get paid."

Jada and Starr were eating at Ra Sushi Bar when Jada said, "I'm in love with a girl."

They were eating sushi and Starr damn near spit her food from her mouth.

"In love with a girl?"

"You know about a week ago Shamari and I met up at Houston's and I told him that I wanted to be with him and I thought that he was the only one that would make me happy and it was the truth."

"What did he say?"

"Basically said he was happy with Ava."

"But what made you realize you wanted to be with Shamari? Do you think it's because Fresh is in jail?"

"No, I've been over Fresh for a while. He played me. He's just like me, but believe it or not, he said that I should be with Shamari. He said he thought I loved Shamari and I do. I don't want him to be with Ava."

"So now you're in love with a girl?"

"I am."

"I don't think you're in love with a girl. I think you can't have Shamari. He's happy so you think that you need someone. Jada, you don't need anyone to validate you. Just be the best version of Jada.

"You sound like one of those a positive-ass Instagram posts."

"I do, don't I? They laughed their asses off. Look, you're confused. You just told me that you went to Shamari and told him how much you loved him and now you tell me that you love a girl."

"I know. It sounds crazy, right?"

"It sounds ridiculous."

Jada laughed and then sipped her drink.

"Who is this girl? Do I know her?"

"Yes."

"Who?"

"Shantelle."

"What the fuck?"

Jada was smiling but Starr was frowning.

"You know how I feel about that girl."

"I know, but I like her."

Starr gave Jada the side eye and then said, "Keep your eye on that girl. She is not to be trusted at all."

Jada understood Starr's disapproval of Shantelle. Shantelle and Starr had slept with two of the same men.

Jada said, "Look, Starr, you're right. I know how you feel about her but you know how I feel about you. You're like a sister to me and if you want me to stop seeing her, I'll cut her ass off. You come first."

"Does she make you happy?"

"She does."

"If she makes you happy, I see no reason to cut her off. But what happens when you want some dick?"

"When I want some dick, I'm going to get some dick."

"See that's how I know you're not really into girls."

"Maybe not, but I'm having fun and I really like Shantelle."

*****

Barry Daniels, along with Agents Mackins and Dumas, had been trailing the UPS driver for the last hour. They'd watched him deliver packages to hospitals, office buildings, and restaurants. Barry received the signal from Mackins that it was time to move in on the driver. The driver strolled back to his truck with a scanner in hand.

Barry and the agents ran at the driver and flashed their badges. "I want the box with the coke in it. Where is it?"

Daniels grabbed B.C.'s skinny ass up by the arm and escorted him into the truck. B.C. yelled and screamed. Hoping someone would see him and come to his rescue.

"You're not going to get me with this bullshit again. I know you're not the Feds. Tell that shit to somebody else."

Barry Daniels placed a Glock .22 against his temple and cocked it. "How about if I blast you in your goddamned cranium if you don't tell me where the coke is? How about that for being real, fuckboy?"

His two white counterparts looked at him and thought that he was crazy because they knew that he was crazy. A hot head.

B.C. bit his lips as he eyed the exit door of the truck trying to decide if he should dash out of the door. "There ain't shit on this truck."

Barry slapped the fuck out of him with the gun. Blood sprayed from the side of his mouth. "The next time, I'm going to kill you, motherfucker. Tell me where the coke is and nobody has to go to jail."

"You're not the real FBI. And there ain't shit on this truck.

Dumas wedged himself between Daniels and B.C. "Look, man, are you willing to die for this coke?"

B.C. thought about his woman and children at home. They were depending on him to come home, but he knew that Stunna was going to kill him if he didn't have his shit. B.C. eyeballed the barrels of the two coal black Glock .22s and decided he'd have to take his chance with Stunna. He turned and gave an eighty-kilo box to the black man. Daniels lowered the gun as he stepped off the truck. He was followed by Dumas and lastly by Mackins.

B.C. fired two shots into Mackins's back and the man crumbled to the ground. Barry Daniels let go of the box and returned fire at B.C., lodging twelve bullets into his chest, killing the man immediately. B.C.'s dead body crumpled on a pile of boxes. Barry Daniels thought about running, but there was no way that he and Dumas could run with that heavy-ass box. Daniels attended to his agent. Agent Mackins had no pulse and a small crowd had gathered.

Barry had no choice but to flash his badge and control the crowd. "Get back. This is official police business."

He radioed for backup. The local police and sixteen more agents from the FBI and the DEA arrived at the scene. The local news wanted him to make a comment but he declined saying that there was an ongoing investigation. The next day they were calling him a hero. He was certain this would help his reputation.

*****

Stunna was taking a nap when he received a call from Micky and he picked it up on the first ring. "Hello."

"Real bad news bruh."

 "What?"

 "B.C is dead. He was gunned down today by the Feds."

"What the fuck are you talking about Mick?   I don't have time for the games Mick."

"I'm serious bruh."

Stunna stood and paced then ran his fingers through his hair and then took a few deep breaths before saying "This is bad Mick, real bad."

"How bad?"

"The biggest lost yet. I've never lost this much."

"What about B.C. what do you want me to tell his girlfriend."

"Fuck B.C. I've lost all my goddamned money I don't give a fuck about him. "Stunna said then he sat back on the bed.

There was an awkward silence, then he said. "You know what Mick I'm sorry. I want you to come to my house I have a couple of watches, I want you to take them and pawn them and give the money to B.C's girl. The watches should bring in close to fifty thousand dollars."

"Why don't you just give her the money?"

"What money?" Mick there is no money. I'm telling you that was big loss. The losses had piled up in the last month and now there was no money and he was in debt to the Russian Connect for over

97

a million dollars. He knew he would bounce back, but how was he going to do it was the question.

Two days later Daniels met TeTe. He hadn't shaved and his beard with long and straggly. He actually looked rather handsome to TeTe.

"You know there was eighty kilos in that goddamned box?" said Daniels.

"Really?"

"Yes. I wish like hell that driver wouldn't have been so brave."

"Don't you mean so stupid?"

"Dumb motherfucker and I had to turn it in."

She smiled. "You're a hero."

"I don't think you understand. I'm just like you. I'd rather have the money. Fuck the accolades, but now maybe they'll get of my ass a little bit."

She felt aroused a little by this handsome black man with this scruffy beard. She'd concluded it was the beard. He was just so goddamned masculine right now.

"So whose shit was that?" Daniels asked.

"I don't know."

"If we're going to work together, you have to tell me what's going on?"

"Look, I told you I'm not naming no names. If you want to get paid, just do what I asked, but I'm not saying shit about nobody."

"Hold up. Let's get one thing straight right goddamned now. I don't work for you. We work together, you understand?"

She was surprised at his cadence. The first couple of conversations she'd had with him, he'd sounded like a cornball. Now he sounded like he was from the hood. Perhaps Daniels wasn't a lame after all.

"OK, we work together but I'm not going to tell you what's going on. No way. You're a cop, man."

"You gotta tell me whose shit it was."

TeTe said, "This was a guy that Black knew. Black had told me the whole ins and outs of the operation. So that's how I knew that the guy was going to have the work."

He gave her a fake smile. "It's what Black knew?"

"Yeah."

"Who is your connect?" Daniels asked.

"I don't have a connect."

"So how do I get my ten percent if you don't have a connect?"

"I don't know."

"Look, I'm going to supply you and we split the money fifty-fifty. Just like me and Black."

"I'm not cut out for the drug business."

"Okay, fine, but you're going to work with me, right?"

"I suppose."

"That's the wrong answer."

She smiled and said, "Yes."

"Fifty-fifty?"

"Yes."

"But before we become official partners…" He paused then narrowed his eyes and said, "I need you to get rid of Jada."

TeTe looked confused. "What do you mean, by taking her out?

"Kill her. I want her dead. Do you understand?"

"Why do you want her dead?"

"Don't worry about it, just do it."

"I can't do that."

"You can and you will. And if you don't, that tip you gave me about the UPS guy? That's called snitching. Do you want to be known as a snitch?"

"Look, I'd given you orders to rob him. I didn't want the man to get killed."

"Doesn't matter. He shot one of my men. I had to turn the drugs in, and now if I tell them who gave me the tip, guess what? Your little street rep is ruined."

TeTe smiled to keep from laughing. "So, you want me to kill Jada?"

"Yes."

*****

Stunna entered the studio. Starr smiled and said, "I didn't think I would ever see you again."

"Why not? We're still friends."

101

"Of course we are, but I didn't think you wanted to be friend-zoned."

"I didn't want to be friend-zoned, but it is what it is. I have to deal with reality and reality is T.J. gets along with Q and you and Q were a couple before we got together."

She smiled and said, "You're a grown-ass man."

He laughed and said, "Plus I'll just keep in touch with you and take on the fallback nigga role."

She laughed and said, "The what role?"

"You know how relationships are nowadays. Everybody has somebody that they call when things ain't going right."

She smiled, revealing her dimples. "So you're going to be my fallback guy?"

"Not fallback guy. Your fallback nigga."

"Boy, you're a mess."

"I'm just keeping it real."

"Did you come by to make me laugh?"

"No, I came by because I got problems."

"What kind of problems?"

"I took a big loss. I mean a major loss. A loss that I don't think I can cover."

"What? What happened?" They sat down on a sofa inside her showroom.

He sighed and said, "Did you hear about the UPS driver that got murdered by the Feds."

"I didn't. What happened?" Then Starr covered her mouth and said, "That wasn't your guy, was he?"

"Yes."

"Oh, man. Damn, I hate that happened. Trey always hated UPS."

"Man, I don't know what could have happened. I don't know who could have snitched. But somebody in my crew said something."

"Do you think Micky could have ran her mouth again?"

He sighed and said, "I don't think it was Mick."

"Who was it?"

"I don't know. I swear to you I don't know I've been around the same group of niggas since I was seventeen."

"So this was consigned?"

"Yes."

"I'm afraid to ask how much."

"It was eighty kilos."

"You've got to be kidding. Who has the balls to ship eighty kilos of coke through UPS? Please tell me that you're kidding. So how many do you owe for? How much was consigned to you?"

"Forty."

"What the fuck?"

"I know. I told my plug and they believe me but they still want their money, so I gotta try to figure out a way to come up with it."

"Damn. I feel so bad for you, babe."

"Babe?" He smiled.

"I can't turn my feelings off for you overnight."

"You remember a few months ago when you offered to loan me some money?"

"Yes, of course I remember. Do you need it?"

"How much is it?"

"I got about fifty thousand I can loan you."

"Damn. I would appreciate that and of course I'll give your money back as soon as I get it up."

"No worries."

"You're the best, Starr."

"Gotta take care of my fallback nigga."

They both laughed.

*****

Shamari and Stunna met up with TeTe at Atlanta Fish Market. She was sitting in a booth toward the center of the restaurant and she was chowing down on Chilean sea bass when they approached.

TeTe smiled and said, "Have a seat and order what you want." Then she turned to Stunna and said, "How did my girl work out for you the other night?"

"She's just a girl. I liked her face, but I like my women with meat on them, you know what I mean?"

"You like big girls?"

"I've been known to knock down a big girl or two, but that's not what I mean. I just like them a little curvier. She was a nice girl, though."

Shamari was confused by the conversation. "What the hell are you talking about?"

"Nothing," TeTe said. She ate a spoonful of creamed spinach and said, "So what's up?"

Stunna leaned across the table and said, "I need your help, and I need it bad. I took a major loss and I ain't got shit."

"Wait a minute. You're the same nigga that said that you don't deal with women?"

"I need you."

"You do realize I'm still a woman, don't you?"

"I'm sorry for what I said. I need you."

She raised her eyebrows and said, "How much did you lose?"

"You don't want to know."

"If I didn't want to know, I wouldn't have asked."

"Eighty kilos."

"Whoa!"

Shamari said, "How?"

"I don't want to even talk about it right now."

"So how can I help you?" TeTe said as she ate another forkful of the sea bass.

"I need consignment. I need whatever you can give me."

"I thought you had money?"

"I was thinking that I could offer you my Maserati, a Range Rover, two pick-up trucks and fifty thousand in cash to use as collateral and you give me twenty kilos. I have to pay these people back and pay them back fast."

"And after you pay them back, I'm sure you're going to cut me off," she said then sipped her water.

"If this works out, we can work together."

"Do you remember how to get to my house?

"Yes."

"Come to my house at eight. Bring the cash. Keep your cars. I'm going to help you make this money back."

"Thanks."

Later that evening, Stunna came over with the fifty thousand dollars in a shopping bag that Starr had given him. TeTe had a suitcase containing twenty kilos of coke.

"Can I at least see the product?"

She frowned and said, "Why? You don't trust me?"

"Of course. I just like to see what I pay for."

She removed one of the packages and grabbed a steak knife from her kitchen drawer. She ripped through the package and he tasted it.

"This is good shit. I can tell."

"Oh yeah, it's good." Then she said, "Look, Stunna, all you got to do is work with me and we'll going to pay off that debt together."

"What do you mean together?"

"Like I told you before. I need you on my team. I'm going to give you these at my price."

"And what's your price?"

"Twenty-two. I'm not going to make a penny off this." TeTe lied but he didn't need to know that.

They made eye contact and for a brief moment she wanted to fuck him. Wanted to see that big dick that Willow had been talking about.

"I really do appreciate this. I swear you don't know how much I appreciate you."

She smiled and said, "It's all good."

He removed a small bag from Neiman Marcus and handed it to her.

"What's this?"

"It's just a small gift to let you know that I appreciate what you're doing for me."

"You don't have to do this," TeTe said. She'd almost felt guilty for having Daniels take his coke, but she knew if he hadn't, they wouldn't be at this point.

She opened the bag and there was a box of Tom Ford Tobacco Vanille perfume. She opened the box then the top of the cologne and sniffed it. "This smells amazing."

He smiled and said, "I'm glad you like it."

He turned and walked toward the door and she yelled out, "Hey, Stunna, can I see it?"

He narrowed his eyes.

Her eyes drifted down to his package. "Willow told me what you were working with."

 He grinned. "What are you talking about? You're crazy."

She ran to the door and blocked the entrance and said, "So what if I'm a little crazy. Just let me see what you're working with."

He unzipped his pants. His manhood was limp but it was still enormous. She covered her mouth and thought it looked like a big black rattlesnake. She kissedthe head and it stood at attention. She lowered her head and took him in her mouth. He stabilized himself against the wall and brushed her hair away from her face, while she sucked him and finally he erupted into her mouth.

The concierge called Q to inform him that Meeka was in his lobby. He told the concierge to send her right up. When she entered the home, she said. "I heard you got your l'il bitch back. You happy now?"

Q was baffled why Meeka and Starr seemed to always be at odds.

Meeka marched right into the living room and set her purse on an end table. Then she plopped down on the sofa.

Q said, "Wait a minute! How long you planning on being here?" The last thing he needed was Starr to come over and find out that Meeka was the one that signed him out on bond.

"Don't worry. I'm not going to be here long." She looked at Q and laughed and then said, "You're one weak-ass motherfucker."

"What do you want?"

"Look, I need five thousand more dollars."

"What?"

"Yes, I need some more money. I'm doing some upgrades to my house and I'm out of money and I was wondering if you would help me."

"Meeka, I've given you fifty thousand dollars."

"I know what you gave me and I damn sure appreciate it brother-in-law, but now I need some more money. Can you help me or not?"

"I can't."

She stood and said, "So you mean to tell me that when I need a favor from you that you can't help me?" She rolled her eyes.

"Yes, Meeka, you did me a favor, but you only did that favor because I paid you."

She grabbed her purse then placed her finger on the tip of his nose. "It's funny how fast motherfuckers forget how you went out of your way to help them."

"I'm sorry you feel that way."

"Damn right I feel that way. You took advantage of me, Q."

"I'm sorry."

"What if I call the motherfucking bondsman to tell them that I don't want to be responsible for you going to court?"

"Do what you want to do."

She rolled her eyes at him and said, "You know what? You're one ungrateful motherfucka." Then she stormed out of the house.

*****

While Ava was at the gym, Shamari was lying on his stomach across his bed scanning Instagram. He wasn't a fan of social media. He didn't believe in posting all of his business out in the public. His Instagram account had three posts. He just liked scrolling through, looking at the half-naked bitches. Most trying to pretend they were proud of their fitness gains, but really they were thirsty hoes trying to get a sponsor and the pics were just a sly way of saying look at my ass; look at what you'll get if you pay my bills.

He had no intentions of paying anyone's bills. He would just rather look for free. He checked out a few of his favorite models before deciding to check out Jada's page. A video of Jada in a backless

110

white dress captioned: DAMN MY BACK LOOKS SO GOOD AGAIN. The damn video had over twenty-eight thousand views. Then there was a picture of her and Shantelle at the Braves game captioned: DATE NIGHT OUT WITH BAE. @NWSHANTELLE. He clicked on Shantelle's page and there were more pics of Jada and Shantelle. At restaurants, at parks, at the gym together.

"Hey, baby, what you doing?" Ava asked him. He dropped his phone then positioned himself onto his back.

 He made eye contact with her and said, "I didn't hear you come in. I thought that you were at the gym."

"I had cramps. So I decided to come home and lay down."

"Damn that sucks."

"Who were you texting?"

"My sister."

"You dropped the phone."

"I did."

"Why?"

"You surprised me."

"Are you sure you were texting your sister?"

"Who else would I be texting?"

"I don't know. What were you texting your sister about?"

"Family stuff."

"Can I see your phone?"

"Can I see yours?"

She chuckled. "So you got something to hide?"

"I ain't got shit to hide."

She walked over to the other side of the bed and attempted to grab up his phone from the floor, but he snatched it.

She stood with her hands on her hips and said, "I know you were texting someone and it wasn't your sister.

"Whatever."

"I hope it wasn't Jada cuz I saw her at the gym the other day with this super fit girl and if I didn't know any better, I would have thought those hoes were carpet munching . I spoke to her and she gave me a half-assed hello, probably mad because I'm with you."

He stood and shoved his phone into his pocket and said, "That's right. You got me, so can you quit being insecure? I wasn't texting anybody that I wasn't supposed to."

"Don't play me, Shamari. Whatever you do, don't play me."

*****

"This guy, Barry Daniels, is a complex man," John said to TeTe, who sat across from him in a booth at Starbucks sipping a mocha latte.

"What do you mean?"

"Everybody I asked about him says he's a superb FBI agent and has won all kinds of accolades, but apparently there is another side to him—a very dark side. There have been several complaints about misconduct and he's under investigation now for misconduct."

"John, this shit does me no goddamned good. Look, how can we take him out? I need somebody. I need that fucking Navy Seal motherfucker that you said you knew to take him out."

112

"I was just telling Stunna that. Honestly, I don't think anybody is going to want to take an FBI agent out."

"I can't deal with him."

"What has he done?"

"He's extorting me and he wants me to work for him. Wants me to sell coke for him."

"What?"

"He's dirty, John. I've been telling you this shit and you don't fuckin' listen to me."

"He wants you to work for him?"

"Yes."

"You don't have to do this. Why don't you just lay low for a while?"

"I can't lay low. I'm in with the cartel now and I just can't quit. I can't just get out of it because I feel like it. It doesn't work like that."

"He knows you're with the cartel?"

"No, not yet. I lied to him because if he knew, he would want ten percent of whatever I make."

"What does he have on you? He has to have something on you to make you feel like you have to work for him."

She looked away from John.

"What does he have on you, TeTe? Tell me."

She set her latte down and said, "Did you hear about the UPS driver?"

"What UPS driver? Wait a minute, the UPS driver that got killed by the FBI? Did Daniels do that?"

"Yes."

"Was that your supply?"

"No, but I told him about the guy. I told him that the work was coming and he was supposed to just take it, but the UPS driver shot and killed one of the agents with him and Daniels fired and killed the UPS driver. Now he's been hailed as a hero."

"Damn."

"I'm surprised your source didn't tell you that."

"They are not going to tell me everything, especially if it's an ongoing investigation."

"Okay."

"You gave him a tip. Why did you do that? I guess he was going to get the drugs and give them to you?"

"Yes."

"But why did you do that?"

"John, always remember that your loyalty lies with me."

"Of course."

"That was Stunna's work."

"Damn, this is crazy as hell. Why did you do that? I thought you were friends."

"I met him through Shamari. I don't really know him. I needed him to be on my team, but he has his own plug and his own work and he didn't want to work with a woman."

"So you dropped a dime on him?"

"That shit sounds old school and it sounds like snitching. The plan was for him to take the box and bring it to me and me and Daniels would split it up. But it didn't work that way."

"Now you're concerned that he's going to let someone know that you were the source."

"Bingo. Now do you see why we have to kill him? And plus he wants me to kill a good friend of mine."

"I'll do my best to help you."

His name was Mikhail Petrov and he was from Moscow, Russia. He was six foot six with blond hair and intense blue eyes. He was a thirty-six-year-old former boxer. Though it had been eight years since his last match, he was still in peak condition. Mikhail and his girlfriend Yolanda, who was a black girl from South Central LA, had just landed in Atlanta. They'd flown in from LAX. He didn't want to be in Atlanta, but he had to come to find out what was going on with his money. He'd shipped eighty kilos of coke to his east coast distributor Stunna-half of it was consignment. The shipment had arrived a month ago and though he'd been in contact with Stunna, he'd yet to receive his money. Stunna had called him a day after the coke was supposed to arrive and the conversation had gone like this.

"I have bad news, Mikhail."

"I like only good news."

"I have a problem."

"What is your problem?"

"My problem is police took the coke and killed the UPS driver."

"You have a big problem."

"I know and I'm trying to figure it out."

"So when are you going to have my money?"

"I don't have the work so I need some product to make some money."

"That is not my problem. Like you started the conversation off by saying that you have a problem."

"I know."

"Get me my money."

"I need an extra two weeks."

"You have extra ten days."

Stunna sighed.

And Mikhail said, "I don't take losses. You know I don't."

"I've been dealing with you for three years and I can't get an extra two weeks?"

"Two weeks it is."

Yolanda had sashayed her sexy little ass to baggage claims and stood by the belt to wait on their Louis Vuitton luggage set.

Mikhail called Stunna and said, "I just arrived. Are you waiting on us?"

"No, I sent my sister."

"The man/girl?"

Stunna laughed. "Yes."

"Is she here?"

"Yes. I'll get her to call you in a few minutes."

"Fine."

Yolanda had gathered all the luggage and Mikhail told her that they'd wait outside for Stunna's sister, Micky.

"I don't see why we can't get our own car service."

Mikhail said, "Please tell me in the last thirty days what have you paid for?"

Crickets.

"Exactly. So shut the fuck up."

"Ever since you heard my brother tell his girlfriend to shut the fuck up, You've worn that phrase out."

Mikhail smiled and said, "I like it."

They stepped outside near the taxi line and Mikhail's phone rang. It was Micky.

"Micky." He tried his best to sound happy to hear from her but the truth was he could care less about her. Actually he didn't give a fuck about her. He hated lesbians but dealing with her was the cost of doing business.

Mikhail and Yolanda climbed into the car with Micky.

Mikhail checked into a suite at the InterContinental on Peachtree and after they were settled, Stunna came over. Mikhail had given Yolanda his Black American Express and Micky took her to Phipps Plaza to go shopping.

Stunna was tall but not tall compared to Mikhail, who stared down at him as soon as he entered the room.

The men shook hands and Mikhail handed him a King of Denmark cigar. Mikhail cut their cigars, then they lit them, even though it was a non-smoking room.

Mikhail said, "You have my money?"

"I don't have it."

He took a pull from his cigar. "This is not what I want to hear."

"You know this is not what I wanted to tell you, but it's the truth. I don't have the money, but I'll get it."

"You told me that a month ago. You asked for two weeks and it has been a month."

"Look, I lost as well. I lost damn near everything I had. At least you have money to fall back on."

Mikhail stared at Stunna with intense blue eyes and said, "So you're counting my money now?"

"No, I didn't mean it like that. I'm just saying that you're better off than I am." He paced and he looked at the big man's huge biceps. He'd brought his gun with him because he knew there was no way that he could beat that man's ass. The man was a boxer and had killed a man in the ring—and in the process had broken both of his opponent's eye sockets. But Stunna would pop his ass if he needed too, but he didn't want violence. He wanted to pay the man, but he didn't have the money.

Mikhail said, "You know how much I like you?"

Stunna was surprised hearing that from Mikhail. He didn't think that Mikhail liked anyone, especially black people. Though Mikhail had a black girlfriend, Stunna still believed that Mikhail was racist and believed that blacks were inferior when it came to intelligence. Stunna dealt with him because he'd given him a hell of a price and he would consign product to him. This had allowed Stunna to accumulate a few million dollars before he'd taken so many losses.

"You like me?"

"I like you."

"Why?" Stunna asked. He was indeed curious.

"I like you because in the past three years, you are the only person I have not had to hurt about my money."

Stunna smiled.

"I'll hurt you if I don't get my money."

"I'm sure."

"I'll kill you if I don't get my money."

"You'll get your money."

"Today is Tuesday, I'm leaving on Saturday and I want my money by Saturday or else I'm going to take your sister with me and every day that I don't have my money I'll cut a finger off."

Stunna laughed. He didn't think Mikhail was serious. He had the money that Starr loaned him and he'd made about a hundred thousand dollars with the product that TeTe had given him, but he was no way near the amount of money that he owed Mikhail.

Mikhail wasn't smiling.

*****

Stunna had called TeTe and she said that she had more product and to bring her money right over. When he entered the house and passed TeTe the money, he was expecting more product.

She said, "I don't have any."

"What the fuck? What do you mean that you're out? You can't be out."

"Look, the plug is coming tomorrow and he's bringing more work. As soon as I get it, I'll call you."

Stunna bit his lips and the palms were sweating.

 She asked, "What the fuck is going on, man?"

He turned and faced her with serious eyes. "Look, my plug is in town and he wants his money and I don't have it. Can you help me?"

"I've already helped you."

"Can you loan me some money?"

"Doesn't he know that you took a loss?"

"He doesn't care about that. All he gives a fuck about is his money."

"Damn! Mexicans can be cold."

"He's Russian."

"Oh damn."

"Look, the product will be here tomorrow night and I'll call you and we can give him the money we make together as soon as we make it."

"I appreciate that. You don't know how much I appreciate what you have done for me."

She grabbed his package and held it for a while, smiled and said, "I'm sure you'll make it up to me somehow."

 He laughed as he left her home.

*****

Monte was surprised when Shantelle had reached out to him to say that she wanted to see him. He promptly added her to his visitation list, and two weeks later, she came to FCI Jessup prison. He'd told all of his homies on the prison yard that one of his baby mamas was coming to see him. Shantelle was a gorgeous woman, so he saw no need to be truthful with them. He'd already told them wild stories about how he used to blow fifty grand a night in the Magic City strip club but they didn't seem to believe him.

Starr had been sending him money every month because she knew that's what Trey would have wanted and some of the inmates still talked about the visit from fine-ass Starr that occurred almost two years ago when Monte had lied like Starr was one of his bitches. He'd even gotten her to pose for a picture with him. So the inmates had all come to the conclusion that Monte must have been some type of high roller. He'd had the paperwork to prove that he'd gotten caught with a shit load of dope and why else would a gorgeous woman like Starr be with an average-looking guy like Monte.

When Shantelle stepped into the visitation room, Monte had this silly-ass grin on his face upon hearing all the oohs and ahhs. She was wearing semi-tight jeans and a long sleeve shirt. The prison didn't allow what they deemed seductive clothing. Monte stood and hugged her. It had been a very long time since he'd seen her. She'd told Trey that he'd lied on the police report but he was still happy to see her—to see anybody from the outside world.

She said, "Looks like You've gained a few pounds."

"Yeah, all I do is work out."

"I didn't mean muscle." She glanced at his stomach.

He laughed and said, "Yeah, but I'm about to get it tight."

"I hear you."

"So what brings you here?"

A tall, ugly-ass dude with bowlegs named Cowboy approached the table and said, "Monte, how about a picture for you and your baby mama?"

Monte quickly cut him off. "Not right now, Cowboy."

Shantelle rolled her eyes at Monte.

When Cowboy was gone, Shantelle said, "Baby mama?"

"Look, just go along with it."

She laughed and said, "You're crazy as hell, Monte."

"Look, you know I didn't have shit when I was out on the street but they don't have to know that."

"I guess not."

"Look, I came here to ask you about a phone."

Monte narrowed his eyes. "What do you mean a phone?"

"Did you have a phone that belonged to Q?"

"No, but he brought me a phone and my cellie got caught with it."

"Cellie?"

"Like roommate but cellmate."

"Oh."

"Yeah, he came to visit me under an alias and I asked if he could bring me a phone. He gave this phone to Officer Harvey, a C.O. that I'm cool with."

"C.O.?"

"You really don't know shit about prison, do you? C.O. stand for correctional officer."

"So he gave the phone to the C.O. who then brought the phone to you?"

"Yes."

"When did he visit?"

"A few days before Trey was murdered. Why?"

"Look, Monte, can I trust you with a secret?"

"You can tell me anything."

Shantelle gave him the side eye. "Monte, I know you're the motherfucker that told Trey about my sister in Florida and told him where he could probably find me."

"I actually told Starr."

"Can I trust you?"

"Yes."

"Q coerced Trey's baby mama to kill him."

"What!" Monte was confused. "How did he do that?"

"Look, the girl was really unstable and he played on that fact. He was texting her from the phone that he'd given you."

"What? Are you saying that he tried to set me up?"

"That's exactly what I'm saying."

Monte tapped the table and bit his lower lip. "Oh, hell no. It's about time for me to get out of this motherfucker. I can't do no more time."

"Look, Monte, don't worry. I'll take care of it. I'm not going to let you go down."

“What are you going to do?”

“I’m going to the police and let them know. I have to. What he’s doing ain’t right.”

Monte wanted to flip the goddamned table over. “Fuck,” he said.

Q rang the bell at Shantelle's place. There was no answer. Then his phone rang. It was Starr.

"Hello?"

"What are you doing?" Starr asked.

"I'm at Shantelle's house, but I don't think she's here."

"Doing what?"

"It's not what you think."

"I know that."

"You do?"

"Yeah, Shantelle has been kicking it with Jada recently."

"What do you mean kicking it?"

"Like how me and you kick it. That's how they've been kicking it."

"Oh, really?"

"Yes. You sound a little jealous."

"Not at all. I'm more surprised than anything else."

"Look, don't go running your mouth."

"I won't say a word. Look, let me call her to see where she's at."

"Okay, call me later."

Q called Shantelle and she told him that she was five minutes away. When he entered her place, he handed her a shopping bag with seventy-five grand in it. But she didn't accept it.

He frowned. "What's wrong?"

"You're trying to set Monte up."

"What the hell are you talking about?"

"Monte told me that you came to see him and you gave him the phone. But you gave him the phone after you texted Jessica and told her to kill Trey."

"What?"

"Look, I don't want the money."

Q just stared at her.

And she said, "Get the fuck out, Q, and I don't ever want to see your face again."

"Did you tell Starr this bullshit?"

"I'm not going to tell that woman shit again. I'm sure she thinks I'm crazy as hell already. Don't worry, she won't find out about your bullshit."

He laughed and said, "You think you got it all figured out, don't you?"

"Look, Q, I need you to get the hell out, right now." She frowned and said, "Go."

*****

The first thing Shamari noticed when he entered Starr's studio was the fine young bitch wearing a mini-skirt.

"Can I help you, sir?"

The young girl was smiling hard with sparkling white teeth. He could see her nipple imprint through the shirt and he could feel

127

himself getting an erection. He'd never thought about young girls before. He never even noticed them, but this little girl was gorgeous.

He said, "Is Starr here?"

"Yeah, she's in the back. Who should I say is here to see her?"

"Shamari."

"I love that name."

"Thanks." He watched her nice little round ass while she strolled to the room to get Starr.

Seconds later, Starr entered the room. She approached him and embraced him. "It's so good to see you."

"Good to see you, too. This is a very nice-ass place you have here."

"Thanks."

Brooke was still standing there smiling at him and Starr invited him to the back. She led him to her office and when he was seated, he asked, "Starr, what the hell is up with Jada and that girl Shantelle?"

"What do you mean, what's up with them?"

"Are they fucking each other?"

"Hey, that's something you gotta ask Jada."

"No, I'm asking you. You're her best friend. You would know."

"You're her best friend."

"It's different between me and her than between her and you."

"Hey, Shamari, that's something that you need to ask her."

Shamari picked up a picture of Starr and T.J. with Goofy. They were at Disney World. He sat the picture back down on the desk and asked, "Is that Trey's son? The one you adopted?"

"Yes."

"You're a good woman, Starr."

"Thanks. That means a lot coming from you."

He stood and said, "I gotta be going. I just thought you would know something, you know? I know Jada has slept with women before, but it's just something about how her and that girl interact just makes me leery. You feel me?"

"Give me an example."

"You know, I was on Jada's Instagram today and just saw a pic that said date night with bae."

"You do realize me and Jada got pictures and we're calling each other bae? Girls do that."

"I know girls can call each other bae. Girls can sleep in the same bed with one another. I know all of that, but I don't know. I have a feeling something ain't right and I think you know about it."

Silence.

"Starr, if you knew about it, would you tell me?"

Starr ignored the question. "What I do know is Jada put her feelings on the line for you. She told you how she felt and how she wanted you back and you shitted on her."

He sat back down. "Tell me how I'm the one that shitted on her? When I got out of prison, I'm the one that wanted to be with Jada. She didn't want to be with me."

"Shamari, you had been gone. She was lonely and she'd formed other relationships. Feelings for other people. You wanted her to cut all of that off right away?"

"No, but I did want to be with her. She is the one that set me up with Ava because she had Fresh. Now that Fresh is gone, she wants to come running back."

"Now that you know that she's with a woman, you want her."

"I just think she deserves better than a relationship with a woman."

"Hey, what's wrong with being with a woman?"

"You wouldn't be with a woman."

"I'm not Jada."

"She deserves better."

"She deserves you, Shamari. Go get your woman if you want her."

Starr stood and hugged him.

*****

Gordo and his crew dropped a large shipment of coke to one of TeTe's homes in Alpharetta. She thanked him and just as he was about to leave, he said. "I have to go up on the price two points."

TeTe frowned and said, "What the fuck do you mean, 'go up on the price two points'?"

"Two thousand dollars."

"Wait a minute. So, let me get this straight. You give me more product and you go up on the price?"

“Yes.”

“Look, you can take this shit and take it somewhere else. I’m not working for free.”

“No, you don’t understand. It is very hard to get right now. It is how you say, dry?”

“Drought?”

“Yes.”

“I don’t believe this shit.”

Then her phone rang. It was Stunna.

“Hey, do you have the work?”

“Yes and no.”

“What does that mean?”

“He’s trying to go up on the price, says it’s a drought.”

“It is. How much is he going up?”

“Two points.”

“Get it. That’s not bad. I have to pay this debt off.”

She terminated the call and said, “I’ll take it.”

“Great and listen, as soon as the drought is over, I’ll go down on the price.”

“Perfect.”

John was at home watching 13 on Netflix when he heard a knock on the door. He jumped up from his bed, slid into some sweatpants, and ran to the door. Through his peephole, he saw a bearded black man that he'd never seen before.

"Yes, can I help you?"

"John Clyburn?"

"Yes."

"Open up. It's the police." The man flashed his badge and John opened the door.

"I'm Barry Daniels of the FBI. Can I speak with you?"

"Of course."

John invited him in and they sat in the living room.

Barry Daniels said, "You're a bad host, John. Aren't you going to offer me some water or coffee?"

John said, "Cut the bullshit. What do you want from me?"

"I heard you been looking for me."

"I haven't been looking for you. Who told you that?"

"You've been asking a whole lot of questions about me."

"So what? That's not against the law."

"What do you want with me?"

"I don't have to tell you shit. As a matter of fact, you can just get the fuck out of my house."

Barry Daniels stood and said, "So did TeTe ask you to do this?"

"What?"

"I know that you know TeTe."

"Get the fuck out of here."

"I don't have to go if I don't want to."

"I'll call the police."

"You don't want to do that because if you do that, I'll just point them to your computer with all the child pornography on your hard drive."

John looked defeated. He knew there was a lot of child pornography on his hard drive. Enough to send him to prison for a very long time. He'd never actually molested a child and he knew it was wrong, but he did visit these underground sites and he liked whacking off to young girls but that was supposed to be his little secret.

Barry Daniels smiled and said, "I did my own background check on you and found out you were fired from the Rockville Maryland police department for whacking off in a high school parking lot."

"Fuck you."

"No, fuck you, perv. And I'm going to tell you something else. You're going to tell TeTe to stop trying to dig up shit on me."

"Okay, I'll stop."

"And just in case you want to delete what's on your hard drive. I already have records of your IP address visiting these sites."

"Look, brother, you don't have to worry about me."

Barry and John shook hands and Barry said, "If I were you, I'd especially get rid of those pictures of Butterfly."

"They are not nudes."

"One hundred and twenty-five pictures of your friend's daughter? That's a little weird, John." He gave him the side eye.

"You asshole. You cloned my phone."

*****

Starr passed Jada a mojito as they sat at Starr's kitchen table. Starr said, "Shamari came by my studio the other day."

"Shamari came by your studio? I didn't even know you and Shamari were that cool."

"You know Shamari used to come by and see Trey from time to time. Not a lot, but he did stop by occasionally."

"Okay." Jada sipped her mojito and said, "What did he want?"

"He wanted to know about you."

"What did he want to know?"

"Was saying that he was on your Instagram and you were hugged up on Shantelle and he wanted to know if you two were fucking around."

"Is that right?"

"Yes."

"What did you tell him?"

"I just shifted the conversation and talked about how I'd heard that you had come to him and admitted your feelings for him."

"What did he say?"

"He loves you."

"Did he say that?"

"No, but why else would he be concerned?"

"Yeah, I think he knows that I'm seeing Shantelle, but he just need some confirmation."

"You know I wasn't about to say anything."

Jada said, "Make me another mojito."

"Look, I made the first one, and you know where the liquor is. Make your own. You ain't no guest."

Jada stood and walked around to the liquor cabinet and made herself a drink. "You know I love that man."

"Why did it take you so long to realize that you love him?"

"I don't know, I just thought that I wanted something else but after time, I realized that nobody is going to treat me like him. I mean it's easy to get guys to buy you things, but me and Mari have a connection beyond material things and beyond sex. His sex is not whack but it's not the best I've had, but still I'll do anything for that man. Anything."

"So if he drops that Ava girl, will you drop Shantelle?"

"Yes, but he's not going to do it."

"I think you need to have another conversation with him. Let him know that you're with Shantelle, but he can change that."

"If Shamari wants me, he'll come and get me. I'm not chasing no man. I've told him that once."

*****

Jada was asleep and then she felt somebody sit on the edge of her bed. She looked up and it was Shamari.

"Boy, what the hell are you doing here?"

"Your garage was open, so I came on in."

"Yeah, something is wrong with my garage door. Sometimes it gets stuck."

"You need to get that checked out. I gotta make a play, so I was just letting you know that I was here."

"You need to call before you come over here."

"Why, your little girlfriend may be over?"

"Hush, boy."

"You so damn country."

"You like it."

"I do." He smiled as he looked at the impression of her ass under the cover.

He asked, "What are you wearing under there?"

"Panties."

"Stop it. You don't sleep in panties."

"Period panties. I'm on my cycle."

He frowned.

"It's not like we were going to go there. You gotta go home to you little girlfriend. Ain't she breaking you off?"

“I don’t want to talk about her.”

He kicked off his shoes and slid under the cover with her and held her. He cuddled her. His dick throbbing against her ass. She liked that.

“Jada, you know I miss you.”

“I heard you were over at Starr’s studio asking a bunch of questions about me.”

“I was.”

“Why didn’t you just ask me?”

“I didn’t think I would get the truth.”

He massaged her ass cheeks and she shoved his hands away. “Stop.”

“You know you like it.”

“But seriously, Mari, what do you think the truth is?”

“I think you and that girl are seeing each other.”

“And if we were, what difference does it make to you? You don’t want me.”

“That’s not true.” His hand massaged her ass cheeks. She didn’t move it this time.

“So you’re with her?”

“No.” She lied. She knew that though he was with someone, he didn’t want to hear that she was with a woman.

“Jada, you and I might not ever be together again, but I don’t want to see you with a woman.”

She said, "Leave, Shamari, you're pissing me off."

"What?"

"Look, you just said that you and I might not ever be together again, so leave. You shouldn't give a fuck who I'm with, if that's the case."

CHAPTER 15

"Did you think about what I asked you?"

"What did you ask? Refresh my memory."

"I want Jada dead."

TeTe paced with her hands on her hips and said, "Look, I know you want me to do this, but I can't bring myself to do that. What did she do that was so bad?"

"I know she's a friend of yours, but I'm going to need you to get someone to take her out. This is not an option."

"So you think you can just pop up on the scene and try to make me trap for you and kill people?"

"We had an agreement and you already broke the agreement."

"What the hell are you talking about? I broke what agreement?" She didn't want to look at him. She sat on her sofa and crossed her legs and he snuck a peek between her legs and he could see her kitty.

"You crossed me already and I don't like that."

"Quit talking in circles. Tell me what the fuck you're talking about. Our agreement was that you were going to get some product and give it to me and we would split the money fifty-fifty."

"That's because you told me you don't have a plug."

"Right."

"But you do."

"I do?"

"TeTe, you didn't think I wasn't going to find out about the big shipment from the Mexicans?"

"What are you talking about?"

"I want my ten percent of the five hundred kilos or kill Jada. One or the other."

"That's not fair."

"Did I say it was fair?"

"How much do you think ten percent of five hundred kilos is?"

"My guess is that you'll make two point five million dollars so I'm looking for two hundred and fifty thousand."

"Your math is way off."

"It doesn't matter. That's what I want and I either get that or you need to take Jada out. I'll give you one week."

"And if I don't?"

"Let's not repeat what happened to Black."

"I loved Black."

"I know you did, but let's just hope you love yourself more."

"Look, I'll do it, but I'm going to need more than a week."

"Did you really love Black?"

"Of course I loved him."

He presented her with a cell phone.

"What the hell is this?"

"The day before Black was killed I met up with him and he left his phone at my office." Daniels lied but he didn't want TeTe to know that he had killed Black.

TeTe looked confused.

Daniels presented TeTe with Jada's text message to Black: "You were amazing last night. I haven't been fucked like that in a long time. Now every time I think of Bryson's Tiller's song "Don't" I'm going to think of you. Come over tonight and finish what you started."

Daniels said. "Now do you think Jada was really your friend?"

TeTe's eyes grew and her heart raced at she read the text. The bitch had fucked Black.

"You have to kill her."

"How can I believe this is his phone?"

Daniels scrolled into the picture section presented several pictures of her and Black and a picture of TeTe's vagina that she sent Black. For a brief moment she was embarrassed that this cornball had a picture of her VJ.

"Any longer than a week, I get my ten percent and Stunna finds out that you tipped us off about his coke. He'll finds out that you ratted."

"I'll do it."

*****

Meeka was sitting in her parent's living room, skimming through ESSENCE magazine, when Starr entered.

"I see you still with ole trifling-ass Q."

"What?"

141

"Don't think I don't know you got back with your man." She laughed then took a swig from a Budweiser and said, "You'll never learn that most niggas aren't shit and especially that one."

Starr looked at her sister and she was very confused about her resentment for Q. As far as she knew, Q hadn't done anything to Meeka.

"Where is Mama?"

"Her and Daddy gone. You know they go to the flea market on Saturday or maybe you don't. You don't come around enough to know what your parents do."

Starr said, "Meeka, what do you have against me? We used to be cool, but now it seems like you are jealous of me for some reason, like you resent me. You were my first hero, my big sis. But every time I come around for the last year or so, it's been these little smartass remarks."

Meeka laughed and said, "What do I have to be jealous of you for?" She sipped her beer then burped. "Oh, because you got a little dope boy throwing money your way. Or is it because you live in a high-rise? Bitch, please. I ain't got nothing to be jealous about with you."

"Let me get out of here before I say something I don't want to."

"Yeah, go running back to no-good Q's house. Motherfucker had Trey killed and you still fucking with him."

"You don't know what you talking about."

"I bet you don't know who got his black ass out of jail."

Starr faced Meeka.

Meeka set her beer down and said, "That's right. I bet you don't know who got his ass out of jail."

"What are you talking about?"

"I got him out. That's right. I got him out and he didn't tell you that, did he?"

Starr frowned and Meeka laughed and said, "Gave yo ass the crying Jordan face, didn't I?"

"You didn't get him out."

Meeka dug into her purse and found a pink piece of paper. She tossed it in Starr's direction. She picked up the document from Mayweather Bondsman and read it. Sure enough, Meeka had signed Q out. Starr crumpled the paper up and tossed it at Meeka then ran out of the house.

Meeka took another swig from her beer, burped, and then laughed her ass off.

*****

TeTe called Jada and asked her if she was going to the protest.

"What protest?"

"Black Lives Matter. Damned state trooper killed another unarmed black man last night. I'm surprised you hadn't seen it on MyFace."

"You mean Facebook?"

"You know I don't know anything about that kind of shit. Anyway, they killed Tavious Miller, father of five, thirty-two years old."

"I'm surprised you are interested in something like that."

"Why?"

"I don't know. You just don't seem like the marching type."

143

"There is a lot you don't know about TeTe. Come on out. Put on some sneakers. It will be fun. It will be like being young again."

Jada wanted to tell the old bitch that she was young, but she didn't want to hurt her feelings.

"Ah, what the hell. I don't have anything else to do." She hung up the phone and called Shantelle and Starr. They both agreed to meet up with her at Five Points. All the women wore sneakers and they marched and carried signs for two hours with the other protestors. They had walked past the CNN center and then back to Five Points. They screamed and shouted at the police just like the younger kids. TeTe even threw an orange, smashing a reporter in the face.

After about two hours, they were tired and they went to the Sundial for drinks. Jada and Shantelle sat on one side of the table and Starr and TeTe sat on the other. They all had strawberry margaritas. Starr had met TeTe before, but this was the first time she'd really gotten to hang out with her and get to know her.

Starr said to TeTe, "You look so young for your age."

TeTe laughed and said, "So I guess I'm supposed to just die in my forties?"

"No, I didn't mean it like that."

Shantelle and Jada held hands under the table.

Shantelle asked, "What is your secret? Honestly, I thought you were about thirty-four. Do you work out?"

"I hate working out."

"You must watch what you eat."

"Not really. I eat what I want. I just don't eat a lot. Some days I might not eat but once. But I love me a good steak."

She sipped her drink and then said, "Jada and Shantelle, are you two together?"

"Yes."

TeTe raised her eyebrows and Jada burst out laughing and said, "Don't look at me like that."

TeTe said, "Like what?"

"Like You've never done a girl."

"I didn't say that I haven't. I done plenty of girls."

Starr said, "Am I the only one at this table that hasn't fucked a girl?"

TeTe said, "Starr, you don't know what you missing."

"TeTe, are you trying to hit on me?"

"No. I don't do friends. I like fucking random girls, but I'd much rather have some pipe." Then TeTe remembered that Starr had been Stunna's girl for a minute.

"What happen to Stunna, Starr?"

"You know Stunna?"

"Yes, met him though Shamari."

"We are better off as friends."

"Really. That is one fine-ass man," TeTe said and the way she said it, annoyed Starr. TeTe sensed it and changed the subject. "Yeah, don't knock something until you try it."

"Try what?"

"A girl."

"I'm not into girls and I don't think I can ever be into girls."

Q called. She sent him to voice mail. She would call him back later.

They sat there and talked for twenty minutes about the first time they'd did a girl. Starr did admit that a girl had stolen a kiss from her before and she was disgusted.

Finally, Shantelle stood and said, "I have to go to bed. I have to work in the morning."

Jada walked her to the elevator of the restaurant and they kissed.

Jada said, "I'll see you later."

Then she made her way back to the table, TeTe was gone.

"Where did TeTe go?"

"Her phone rang and she went to the bathroom."

TeTe was inside a bathroom stall talking to Daniels.

"Hey, I need this to happen tonight," Daniels said.

"I don't work for you. We work together."

"Just make sure it happens."

TeTe terminated the phone call then she walked back to the table where Starr was texting and Jada was posting a video on Snapchat.

Jada looked up from her phone and said, "I'm going to ride with Starr. I'll call you later this week. We gotta get out and do this again."

TeTe raised her eyebrows. "So you spending the night with Starr?"

"No, not at all. We've decided to stop by and see our deceased friend Lani's mom. She's like a second mom to both of us."

TeTe gave them a fake smile and said, "Good to see you again, Starr."

The women hugged.

Jada's garage was open and he walked right in, tiptoeing into the bedroom. Shantelle was sound asleep her gold and blue silk scarf covering her head. He picked up the extra pillow and covered her face. She screamed but the pillow muffled her voice. He fired three shots into the pillow blood from her head turned the white pillow crimson and sprinted through the garage, hopped into a Honda Accord Hybrid and drove away.